Bounty Hunters' Range

**Center Point
Large Print**

**This Large Print Book carries the
Seal of Approval of N.A.V.H.**

Bounty Hunters' Range

Lauran Paine

Center Point Publishing
Thorndike, Maine

This Center Point Large Print edition
is published in the year 2005 by arrangement with
Golden West Literary Agency.

The text of this Large Print edition is unabridged. In other
aspects, this book may vary from the original edition. Printed in
Thailand. Set in 16-point Times New Roman type.

ISBN 1-58547-614-5

Library of Congress Cataloging-in-Publication Data

Paine, Lauran.
    Bounty hunters' range / Lauran Paine.--Center Point large print ed.
      p. cm.
    ISBN 1-58547-614-5 (lib. bdg. : alk. paper)
      1. Large type books. I. Title.

PS3566.A34B69 2005
813'.54--dc22

2005001157

Chapter One

Where the sun sank, leaving behind a red-streaked sky, was a narrow slot in the Cheyenne Mountains. Downward and outward from that slot was the endless-seeming broad, rich plain of Cheyenne Valley.

Cowmen had been saying for fifty years there was no better uplands browse, nor no better flat-land graze, in all the Territory of Wyoming, than Cheyenne Valley. Even the riders who'd worked that big valley, the lowland, piney foothills, and the snake-like twists and bends of Indian Creek, which ran from north to south, more or less, or from the mountains to the north down across Cheyenne Valley and out of sight down through the far-away black-rock, forbidding shapes of the low and bulky canyons of the Purgatory Hills, said they'd never seen such a cow empire. They said it in awe and in admiration. They didn't often say it in envy because no one man, no matter how smart he was or how dedicated to acquiring a cattle domain equal to many of Europe's duchies in size, could have hoped to have owned, in one lifetime, all the lands that comprised the Burcham ranch, lock, stock, and barrel.

From the Cheyenne Mountains to the Purgatory Hills; from the westering Laramie River to the easterly town of Gatling; no one knew how many acres, and the Burchams figured it in miles and leagues. The estimates ran from a hundred thousand acres to five hundred thousand. The nut-brown, lanky men up from the *Llano Estacado*—the Stakes Plains of Texas—said warn't no point in working for the small outfits; that Texas-men just naturally belonged where the sun never set, where a man could be a week riding betwixt the front door and the back door, and where the power that was money, stood four-square behind the dark force of violence.

The Texans were right. Power had no teeth unless it also had retainers. Ten Texas-men under Lysle Small stood ready to support and enforce, at the drop of a hat, any Burcham edict. Rolled together, Burcham power and Texan force, were enough. They'd been enough for forty years and more. Old Jared Burcham who'd wrung his cow empire from the fiercest of warrior tribesmen, the Northern Cheyenne, whom even the redoubtable Sioux feared, laid down a law that far back: 'Hire Texans. Others may be as good, sometimes, but Texans are *always* dependable. Hire Texans and Cheyenne Valley will be ours down to the last generation of us!'

Old Jared had hired Texans. Their names and initials were carved deeply into the logs of the big home-ranch bunkhouse. Also, the years were carved there, starting before Wyoming was more than a local name among Indians, on down to when Wyoming became a Federal Territory. By then Jared was gone, buried in the family plot atop a low hill west of the home-place, imprisoned, along with his wife and two children who hadn't survived childhood, behind the black-iron wrought fence.

More Texans came during Jared's son's time. Virgil Starr of Adobe Walls, Clay Allison of El Paso, Jack Plummer of Houston, Jefferson Davis Munroe of Hasyampa, who could draw and fire just as fast with his left hand as with his right.

Like Jared's son, whose name was Enoch, they were all gone; only the legends, the carved initials, the abbreviations for the years, lingered to even show that they'd once ridden Burcham range.

But the old man's remembered edict still lived: 'Hire Texans.' Lysle Small hired on four years after Jared's son Enoch was planted up there on the low hill behind the wrought-iron fence, by Enoch's son and daughter, the second Jared, named for his grandfather, and the second Samantha, named for her grandmother, who'd been the first Jared's cherished wife.

Lysle Small was a pale-eyed, square-jawed man with no outward characteristics to set him apart from other men. He'd been born down along the Canadian River, had teethed on Spanish spurs and Mex saddles, had killed for the first time at sixteen and had gone up the trail at eighteen with a reputation for being quiet and unsmiling and deadly. He'd worked the Montana ranges for two years then had drifted down into Wyoming Territory, aged twenty years. For three years he'd labored over around Fort Laramie, had married in his twenty-fourth year—she'd died the following Fall in childbirth—and at twenty-five he'd drifted to the town of Gatling where Jared Burcham had seen him, hired him on, and now, four years later, at twenty-nine,

Lysle Small was rangeboss of everything he could see in all directions, including ten more Texas-men like he also was.

But the Territory had changed considerably since Old Jared's time. The awesome and terrible Northern Cheyenne were vanquished. Their nearly as fierce Sioux allies had been hounded and battled and decimated and finally rounded up, herded like dumb-brutes onto reservations, and were beginning their tragic comeback into the brotherhood of Man, now ruthlessly ruled by pale-eyed men with alien ideologies.

Redskin marauders passed their secret trails to the lawless night-riders; the scheming, cruel and ruthless whiteskins whose savagery had a different twist to it, and whose methods, while not often very different, at least had something less exalted than pure survival as the end result.

Lysle Small had hanged—and John Wheaton *knew* he'd hanged—no less then seven horse and cattle thieves, in the secret and gloomy places throughout the foothills of the Cheyenne Valley range, in his four years at the Burcham ranch. But John Wheaton was as much a product of his times as Lysle Small also was, even though John had come originally from flat Kansas, where the rules were different than rules were in post-war Texas.

A horsethief was the lowest of criminals; a cowthief was scarcely any better. It was habit to lynch them where they were taken, and habit, if permitted to go unchecked, soon becomes a tenet of environment.

John Wheaton was the law of Cheyenne County, with headquarters at the town of Gatling. He knew Lysle Small as well as he knew graying and thin-lipped Jared Burcham, or Jared's younger but equally as iron-hard handsome sister, Samantha. John did not interfere. Not that he feared the Burchams or Lysle Small. He didn't. John Wheaton feared no man—or woman. But John Wheaton's world had two sets of law, equally as dedicated to the preservation of peaceful, law-abiding existence for everyone: Book-law and gun-law. As far as he knew neither one was any more capable of injustice towards the common good, than the other, which was good enough for John Wheaton.

But men are as their times only—*during their formative years*—and those years fade out, become altered and different and alien to life as it should be lived long before the men they've formed and sustained have reached full maturity, so, for men like Jared Burcham and Lysle Small, and John Wheaton, conviction and loyalty and dedication to a way of life is always a little *passé,* a little old-fashioned, even before they've reached full manhood.

It is *the* curse of mankind that between boyhood and manhood everything completely alters including men's faiths and convictions and solidest convictions, without the enforcers of a particular out-moded way of life ever actually knowing that this is so.

Whether life and environment change for better or worse isn't the point. Men fiercely defend that which has formed them against that which they neither under-

9

stand nor really even believe has come to replace old ways and systems, and here, in a sentence, is the crux of all strife and tragedy, in the world, in the nation, or in Cheyenne Valley where Jared Burcham ruled from his galleried big white-painted ranch-house, and where Lysle Small stood thick-thewed on the log bunkhouse porch smoking his evening cigarette, lord, in his own lesser way, of all he surveyed.

Old Phil Chandler, the saddle and harness maker over in Gatling, who remembered Old Jared when both had been young men, and had seen the whole country change again and again, put it this way to Frank Arbuckle, who owned and managed the big mercantile establishment in the center of town, who also could remember a long time back.

'Time was, Frank, when, if you'n me rode out to get some camp-meat an' seen a redskin, we just snuck up and burst a cap on him as a natural thing, flung him in a crevice in the rocks along with his cussed feathers and beads and medicine-pouch, flipped a coin for his weapons an' his horse, then come on home.

'Now; if a man shoots a redskin the law's after him like a herd of turtles after a sand-fly. That's how things've changed.

'A man's got a lot of things to put up with an' abide by nowadays that warn't figured to be bad at all, forty year' back.'

Frank could agree with that, but from a different point of view. 'Time was,' he dourly said, 'when a man owed me a bad debt, I just took m'guns and rode to his camp and told him I'd come for one o' three things: M'money that he owed me, his horse an' outfit if he didn't have the danged money—or his life, if he wanted to make a fight of it.'

Phil looked across his cutting table, bemused. 'An' now?' he said.

Frank Arbuckle snorted. 'I file a lien. Eight times out of ten he's got nothing, so I lose out an' the law sympathizes with me. Sympathy? Phil; I got a cellar full of sympathy. The law says if I take a gun an' go throw down on the deadbeats, I'm in the wrong, I'm breakin' the law, I'm a blasted criminal. An' the deadbeat stands up in court smilin' right into my face and accuses me of intimidation. I get fined an' maybe put under bond, but the worst thing is, Phil, the folks I've known for thirty, forty years, look at me like I'm some kind of a villain.'

It wasn't an exaggeration, any of it. That's how much Wyoming Territory had changed in the forty or fifty years since Old Jared and his kind had ridden into the savage country with a gun in one hand, a dream in the heart, a Bible in one pocket, and the moral conviction that men of strong will and courage were entitled to take, and to hold, all they could decently cultivate, keep orderly, and make contribute to the common prosperity.

But as soon as the land had been secured by them, and their blood and their sweat, it began changing again, as it always had and as it always would. None of the old-timers liked what change they saw; none of them envied nor hated nor wished evil for the Burchams. In their simple eyes Cheyenne Valley was the great stabilizing influence in Gatling, in all their round-about environment. But the old-timers were few and getting fewer, while new faces, new blood, and new ideas, infiltrated the land.

Carleton Whitsett who came initially to buy horses for the Army, and who'd stayed on to buy cattle, and eventually, some isolated parcels of land, was one of the first to say no man had a right to own so much land or to control so much wealth. In Old Jared's day such heresy would have brought a night-visit, a warning, and perhaps, if the warning were ignored, a bullet.

But this was forty and more years later. Folks were uneasy, it is true, in the face of such an outspoken, unheard-of statement, but they did nothing, and of course there were some who, for the first time, wondered if maybe what Carleton Whitsett had called 'despotic feudalism' wasn't in fact, just exactly that.

Gatling, though, was a cow-country village. Carleton Whitsett's type was new to it. Although he met the cattlemen and rangeriders in the *Antlers*, which was Gatling's best and biggest saloon, patronized by cowmen and the more substantial townsmen almost exclusively, he was different from them. Not in dress nor speech, particularly, but in his way of smiling—or not smiling—and in his way of talking and acting. Carleton Whitsett was from San Francisco down along the California coast; in comparison to the men of the Gatling country, he was worldly and smooth and capable; he wore Prince Albert coats and didn't carry a gun; at least he carried no visible gun, like everyone else did. The women thought him polished and handsome and he was both. But what neither the women nor the men knew nor even suspected at first, was that Carleton Whitsett was cruel and ruthless and predatory. Moreover, he'd reached that stage in his life which all men sooner or later arrive at; he wasn't satisfied with himself. He wanted to achieve things, and fast.

Chapter Two

As all wise men know, the way to reach down for the support of people is to appeal to their selfishness. Not to what is best for them because not one out of ten men on earth really know what's best for them, but to appeal to their cupidity, their avarice, their greed, and their secret passions.

Cheyenne Valley was huge; it was rich and green and well-watered. It could be the nucleus for a hundred or more large ranches owned by individual men, not just one unmarried brother and sister who'd acquired it through blind inheritance.

'Look how they live,' Carleton Whitsett told the men at the *Antlers* bar. 'Look how those swaggering Texans stride up and down your sidewalks and ride into your herds looking for Big B cattle; like they're gods and the rest of us are nothing. Do you have any idea how rich a hundred or two hundred separate cattle spreads would be, carved out of Burcham holdings? How much more money would come to Cheyenne Valley and get spent right here in Gatling? Boys; there'd be schools, and buggyworks to hire men, theatres even, like they have down in San Francisco. This wouldn't be a lousy little cow town stuck on the far edge of one huge ranch picking up whatever scraps those Burchams in their big white house wanted to throw our way. Gatling would rival Denver or Salt Lake City, or, in time, maybe even San Francisco. . . . And you listen to me, men: For those who owned the land which would be needed as Gatling grew and expanded, there would be hundreds of thousands of dollars!'

Frank Arbuckle told John Wheaton, his faded eyes dark with indignation, 'If someone doesn't shut that man up, John, he's going to cause some bad trouble around here.'

Wheaton's reply was practical. 'What's he done? Hell, Frank; this here's a free country. A man can spout off, there's no law against it.'

Arbuckle went down to the saddle shop, had a cup of coffee with Phil Chandler and bristled with imprecations. 'He's deliberately tryin' to suck the Burchams into a fight with the town, Phil. He's linin' folks up with him, against Jared and Samantha Burcham. I told John Wheaton he's going to make real trouble, and I tell you that for a fact. I know his kind; smooth, crooked as a dog's hind leg, scheming, sly as a snake. Mark me, Phil; he'll get folks to his way of thinking. He knows all the tricks, too.'

'What tricks?' asked the saddle and harness maker. 'When a man goes up against the Burchams, Frank, he'd sure-Lord better know a lot of tricks. I'd as lief have the Devil himself on my trail as have Lysle Small for my enemy. Or those string-bean Texans he has at his back. I tell you what I figure, Frank: One of these days Lysle and Jared will hear of this feller's talk.' Old Phil Chandler rolled up his eyes. 'That'll be that. Mister San Francisco Whitsett'll just saddle up and ride on, an' never come back, or he'll just drop out'n sight.'

But Frank Arbuckle thought otherwise and said so. 'Phil; Jared or Lysle can't just do like their pappies and grandpappies would've done. You just can't ride up to a man any more and call him out into the center of the roadway. Just the other day we were talkin' of how things'd changed. I tell you they can't just shoot that man for talking. It's up to John Wheaton to run him out of town.'

'How?'

'How? How the hell do I know—how? I'm telling you just what I told John: Unless someone does something there's going to be bad trouble. Now I've got a business to think of, so have you an' the other merchants of Gatling. If John doesn't do something right quick it'll be up to us to call him before the Town Council and *make* him do something.'

After Frank had departed, Phil Chandler had a second cup of coffee and wondered, with all the restrictions against direct forceful action nowadays, just what could be done. Not that Carleton Whitsett's talk had disturbed Phil at all. It hadn't. But the primary reason it hadn't was because Phil had never heard it first-hand,

15

and it had been nearly fifty years since he'd prejudged a man on hearsay. He quit doing that about the same year he quit chasing women. Usually, that's about how long it takes a man to get some sense, in both those departments.

But there was another reason for Phil to hold off; he'd known Frank Arbuckle as long as both of them had been in the Gatling country, which was to say before Gatling was a town and before Wyoming was a Territory. Frank was shrewd; he'd always had a nose for business whether trading with redskins for their winter-trapped furs, or with the army when unhorsed dragoons had needed remounts, or, as now, with a business that spanned two counties, operated three freight wagons, and was housed in the largest building in town, with a long, log warehouse out back.

Frank was shrewd and careful and mighty clever in his own line, which was trading, but he also happened to be irascible, short-tempered, and quick to judge. Therefore, Phil downed his second cup of java, returned to his cuttingtable and resumed laying out the template for the new saddle he was making, thinking that perhaps Frank was making a mountain out of a molehill. After all, knowing a man fifty years helped sometimes in arriving at correct evaluations of his statements. Or at least it *should* have.

For John Wheaton, though, who'd heard Whitsett make his trouble-talk and who'd also had to weather several stormy sessions with Frank Arbuckle, the issue wasn't so much what Carleton Whitsett said, as it was what would happen when that talk got back to the Burchams. John was a man in his mid-forties who'd come through a lot of storms, verbal and otherwise. He wasn't a complicated man at all; he was direct and frank and unassuming. He also just happened to be a dead shot with either hand, with six-gun, carbine, and derringer.

But John was by nature rather calm and philosophical, which was to say he was lazy. He meant to ride out to the Burcham place and have a talk with Jared, but he kept putting it off. In fact, he put it off until it was too late, because after about three weeks Carl Whitsett's talk had gone all over the countryside.

John and Abner Folger, who owned the *Antlers Saloon* and was a heavily-made man with hands like hams and big blue eyes as round and soft and pleasant as the eyes of a baby, had a habit of playing whist or pinochle or, less often, stud-poker, in the pleasant summertime evenings, over at Abner's saloon. In fact, their particular table, over in a far corner out of the mainstream of the bar-traffic, was known to be more or less reserved just for that traditional evening game. Only strangers ever took that table, and even then they only did it if the bartender didn't happen around to chouse them away before sundown.

But occasionally it happened that when John came over after supper to play, there'd be some uninformed saddle-tramp or peddler seated at the table enjoying a drink or just drowsing. When that happened John'd explain about the table and shoo the interloper off, which would be the end of it.

One night it didn't work that way. There were two of them, unshaven, rawhide-men with the closed-down visages and the sulphurous, steady eyes of gunfighters, at that table. John made his appraisal of those two as he strolled on over. Gatling often got that type, but ordinarily they only remained overnight. Gatling didn't have much need for gunfighters. In fact, it didn't have *any* need for them.

John explained about the table, the gunfighters listened, and in the ensuing silence which stretched out to its maximum limit, the strangers took John Wheaton's measure exactly as he'd taken theirs. John wasn't a tall, hawk-like individual with smoldering eyes; he was a very average looking ex-cowboy running a little to lard around the middle. He had thick, sloping shoulders, long arms, and scarred hands. He also had a square jaw, a long-lipped mouth, and very steady eyes. He might have fooled a lot of average men, but to gunfighters whose very survival depended upon making the right assessment the first time, he wasn't quite as he looked.

The pair of gunfighters got up and ambled over to the bar. They didn't say a word to Sheriff Wheaton; even after they were slouching over the bar they didn't look back at him.

In time Abner showed up, flagged his barman for the two beers-on-the-house which invariably accompanied their evening game, and sat down. With a grunt as he settled his solid bulk comfortably, Abner said, 'Sweet pair you ran off, John. Gunfighters?'

Wheaton reached for the cards to shuffle them and nodded his head. 'We get our share, but I reckon you're the only feller in town who ever profits much off 'em. What d'you say to making a change tonight, Ab; what d'you say to a little draw poker?'

Folger shrugged thick shoulders. 'Suits me. Nothing wild, Jacks or better to open, and a penny-ante game.'

Carleton Whitsett entered the saloon. John saw him pass to the bar as he was lifting his cards close to his chest. Whitsett was a handsome man, always clean looking and freshly shaved. Somewhere down the line he'd picked up more than just an ability to buy and sell livestock profitably; he'd also learned how to make an entrance. He could walk into Abner's saloon when the place was full of rangemen, smoke and noise, and somehow catch almost everyone's attention.

He even had a way of calling for a drink at a crowded bar that made it seem he was somehow instilling culture into the saloon, and that wasn't easy in a land where every man drank and also banged the bartops for his liquor.

Wheaton forgot about Whitsett. Abner, with his back to the bar, didn't even know Whitsett was over there. He couldn't have possibly cared less, either, for the first few hands, because the cards were showering him with good fortune.

But when Lysle Small and four of the Burcham Ranch Texans walked in, Abner, whose mature lifetime had been spent in the saloon business, felt the subtle chill come into his saloon and twisted around in the chair to see who had just come in out of the warm evening, or what had occurred to make the atmosphere change in a way that only a seasoned barman could sense.

Lysle Small was a little like John Wheaton where appearances fell short of giving a true and accurate picture of the man; Lysle was slightly under six feet, broad-shouldered, narrow-hipped, pale-eyed and thin-lipped. He wore a tied-down gun, but then so did eighty percent of all the men who rode the range in the Cheyenne Valley country. His clothing was no different from that of his riders, and because he was a soft-spoken, taciturn man, he didn't seem dangerous. At least he didn't *act* dangerous nor look the part.

But again, when those two gunfighters hunching over the bar turned to quietly study the Burcham Ranch men, they weren't fooled by Lysle or the lean-flanked, sun bronzed men with him. Ab could tell by the way those two gunfighters turned back to their drinks that they'd read Lysle Small right. Neither of the gunfighters smiled nor showed in any way they were scornful of the five newcomers along the bar.

Carleton Whitsett eased aside to give Lysle and his men elbow room. Whitsett too, made a particular point of not looking at the Burcham Ranch men, but with Whitsett the mood was different; he was being prudent and aloof and definitely cool.

Lysle nodded at Abner's night barman, who promptly set up a bottle and five glasses. The Burcham riders were engrossed in their serious drinking for a while, looking neither right nor left. As a rule, though, they weren't too familiar with the other cowmen or townsmen anyway, so no one paid much attention to them now. They had their strictly Burcham Ranch way of doing things. They stepped on no one's toes and no one stepped on their toes; it wasn't exactly an amiable arrangement, but it worked well enough.

The catcher, though, was that this exact attitude on the part of the Burcham Ranch men was what had initially given Carleton Whitsett his opening among the townsmen and rangeriders. Small and Jared Burcham, he'd said many times, and their riders, rode the roads and trod the sidewalks as though they owned the Universe. They looked down on everyone else. They entered the corrals of other ranchers looking for Big B beef, and they did it as though there was no law greater than Burcham law.

They were acting the same way this night, too, but John and Abner Folger were not concerned. Not at first anyway. Not until Lysle Small stepped back from the bar, rapped Carleton Whitsett on the back, and when Whitsett turned, blasted a sledge-hammer strike into Whitsett's face that splattered Whitsett's blood over the two gunfighters and several other astonished spectators along the bar.

Then Lysle turned, with his four men, and walked back out of the saloon.

Chapter Three

They were waiting out there beside their Big B horses at the tie-rack in front of the saloon when John Wheaton came angrily through the louvered doors. They looked straight over at him, impassive, tough-eyed, resolute.

John slowed at the plankwalk's very edge and fixed Lysle with a cold look. 'You're under arrest for assault,' he said. Then, in a slightly different tone he said, 'Would you mind tellin' me what that was all about?'

Lysle didn't mind in the least. 'Talk, John. That man's been talking against the Burchams. He's been hanging around Gatling for nearly a month now, trying to line up some support for whatever he's got in his crooked mind. We heard about it a couple of weeks back, but we figured he'd be moving on. There isn't much here for his kind. Then we learned he's been buying little isolated tracts of land here and there—reselling them, or at least trying to resell them at cost, by advertising them in Denver and Laramie and San Francisco newspapers. He's trying to stack the deck, John; bring in his own people to make war against Big B.'

Wheaton hadn't heard about the land scheme. It made him stand and ponder for a moment. Meanwhile, several of the barflies who'd been inside and had seen

Whitsett knocked senseless, drifted on out, full of curiosity about what would happen next. The pair of slouching gunfighters were there among them, leaning on the darkened front of the *Antlers*, stonily looking and listening.

John didn't have much choice. 'Be all that as it may,' he told Lysle. 'You're under arrest for assaulting Mister Whitsett.' He stepped down off the plankwalk. 'Come on, Lysle. Your boys can go back and tell Jared, but you're goin' to spend the night in jail.'

Lysle didn't offer any objection. He handed the reins to his horse to one of his men with orders for the critter to be stabled at the liverybarn down at the lower end of town, turned and went along with John Wheaton.

That was the end of it. At least that was the end of that particular phase of it. Several sympathetic rangemen helped Carleton Whitsett over to Doc Bean's dispensary where he was patched up, and except that Gatling, and all the cow-camps for miles in all directions, had a fresh topic of gossip to chew over, the episode ended when Jared appeared in town the following morning early, paid the five dollar disturbing-the-peace fine levied by Justice Court Judge Garry Hollar, and didn't show by gesture nor expression whether he approved or disapproved, as the two of them loped back out of town.

But four days later when the stage arrived, a thin, dark-eyed, hungry looking man in his late twenties or early thirties got off, carrying a satchel and a briefcase, took up residence in an upstairs room of the Gatling

Hotel, and prepared a paper which he later took across to the jailhouse and handed to John Wheaton, saying, 'Sheriff; I'm Charles Korngold, attorney for Mister Carleton Whitsett. That paper I've just given you is to be served upon Jared and Samantha Burcham, Lysle Small, et al. Their notification that suit for damages has been instituted against them in the sum of ten thousand dollars, for grievous injury to my client, Mister Whitsett.'

John sat at his desk looking up at Charles Korngold as though he didn't believe either his eyes or his ears. Finally he put the paper down and looked at it the same way. He'd been a cow-town law officer most of his later life; he'd seen lawsuits before, but not for ten thousand dollars and not because someone took one hard punch in the nose. Then he sighed and stood up and said, 'You're serious, aren't you?'

Korngold bobbed his head up and down. 'Dead serious,' he answered.

John nodded. 'I thought so. Well, Mister Korngold, you'd better be just serious. Bein' *dead*-serious in this country can end up with you bein' more of one than the other.'

Charles Korngold's dark-liquid eyes clouded up with perplexity. 'No riddles, please,' he murmured. 'Was that some kind of backwoods threat, Sheriff?'

'Why no, Mister Korngold. It was more in the nature of a damned promise,' replied John Wheaton, taking up the paper and dubiously eyeing it. 'An' in case you're interested, this paper's going to make Carl Whitsett the

24

laughin' stock of the range country. A man doesn't sue over a punch in the nose. Every cowboy for a hundred miles around'll be laughin' fit to bust by tomorrow night, when this gets out. Whitsett's goin' to look about as ridiculous as a man can look. This here is the town of Gatling, Wyoming Territory, Mister Korngold, not San Francisco or Denver. Little things like punches in the nose aren't squared up by anything as silly as this.' John waggled the paper under the taller and younger man's slightly hooked nose. Then he broadly smiled. 'But I'll deliver it. I'll take it out to the ranch right now. Jared an' Lysle'll be duly notified by sundown. It takes that long to get to the Burcham home-ranch. After that, they'll probably round up their Texans and come ridin' into town.'

Wheaton stuffed the paper into a pocket and went after his hat. Lawyer Korngold stood his ground watching everything John did, but when the sheriff opened the door to step out into the pleasant mid-day sunshine, Korngold said, 'Sheriff; just a second.' He went outside with Wheaton, looked up and down the dusty, drowsy roadway, lowered his voice and said, 'Frankly now, and in all honesty between two men whose profession is the law and its due enforcement— what will happen tonight?'

John spat into the roadway dust, squinted up his eyes and drawled. 'Well; maybe another lawsuit for another ten thousand, Mister Korngold, for another broken nose. Yours.' He brushed his hatbrim with one hand, turned and went striding down towards the liverybarn.

It usually took between ten and fifteen minutes for a man to get his horse saddled and led out, depending upon how busy the liverybarn attendants were in the middle of the day, so, after passing the order for his mount to be rigged up and led out front, Sheriff Wheaton lounged in the doorway gazing back up the roadway. He saw Charles Korngold pace up and down out front of his jailhouse-office for a few moments, then turn and hike in a bee-line straight for the stage-line office and rush in, up there, out of sight.

John Wheaton grinned, took his horse when it was brought forth, swung into the saddle and loped out of town by the back way. He'd already put off talking to Jared and Samantha Burcham too long; he'd kept intending to ride out there. But it was a long ride to make in one day, put him back in Gatling well past his accustomed supper time, and it spoiled his chances for getting back some of the money Abner had won off him the night before. But aside from all that, he just plain didn't cherish reproving Jared.

Of course, with that paper in his pocket, reproving anyone was pretty well taken out of his hands. Whether Korngold left Gatling on the next stage or not wasn't going to resolve much. Carleton Whitsett *had* instituted a lawsuit, and even though John didn't expect him to press it, nevertheless the Burchams—and Lysle Small—were going to become pronounced enemies of Carleton Whitsett tonight, which meant trouble exactly as Frank Arbuckle had been predicting.

John rode across the broad expanse of Cheyenne

Valley looking with an old professional's skeptical interest at the Big B cattle and horses he passed. They were tallow-fat and shiny-hided. When he halted to water his horse at the meandering creek he flushed two doe-elks, barren and blue-coated. Splashing on across he sent trout-minnows scurrying in all directions, and sighed with a fisherman's wish that he'd had a pole along.

Then he spotted the solitary rider atop a low knoll watching his progress, and for a time ignored that unmoving silhouette up there. The Burchams had always been jealous guardians of their immense domain. Old Jared, forty, fifty years back, had taken his bristling-armed cowboys down more than once to turn back migrating redskins, and later, migrating white-skins with white-topped wagons. In Enoch's day there'd been an incident or two, also, but now, in the day of the second Jared Burcham, it wasn't necessary, really, nor even profitable, to keep armed cowboys patrolling, if that's what the rider atop the knoll was about.

Finally, annoyed a little at that motionless surveillance, Sheriff Wheaton swerved his horse and headed straight for the knoll. The rider finally moved; reined down off the hill and walked straight up to him. When they were still two hundred yards apart Sheriff Wheaton saw his mistake. It wasn't a Big B cowboy at all, it was Samantha Burcham. She was wearing a cream-colored blouse with long sleeves that she filled out admirably, and was otherwise attired in a rusty, long riding skirt which covered the uppers of her heavily and ornately hand-stitched boots.

Samantha was a handsome woman. She was no longer a girl. She was, John Wheaton thought, either in her early thirties or very close to them. He knew for a fact she was a good twenty years younger than her brother, Jared, but the trouble was, Sheriff Wheaton didn't know how old Jared was.

Not that it made a bit of difference; Samantha was full-figured and solid as rock when she moved. She had cascading coppery hair that fell half way down her back, large blue eyes, a full-lipped mouth, rather wider than most, which was a Burcham characteristic, and she also had something else which went with the Burcham name: Iron.

It was said the reason Samantha Burcham had never married was because she'd never yet run across a man she couldn't out-ride, out-shoot, or out-stare. When she halted and lowered her reins to look straight at John Wheaton with those unflinching blue eyes, now, John sighed. No doubt about it, Samantha Burcham was a beautiful woman. Even more handsome now in the fullness of her full maturity, than she'd been as a girl.

'Heading on up to the home-place,' he said to her. 'Got a legal paper to serve on you folks and Lysle. Seems Carleton Whitsett is suing all of you for damages because Lysle punched him in the face in Abner's saloon.'

'Damages,' said Samantha. 'What kind of damages, Sheriff?'

'Ten thousand dollars worth, Samantha.'

The unwavering blue eyes got round with astonishment. For a moment Sheriff Wheaton thought Samantha was going to swear or shake a fist, or maybe even faint, but she didn't do any of those things; she laughed.

John smiled, feeling silly out there with that paper in his pocket for such a ridiculous reason. He waited for the mirth to subside then he said, 'Is Jared home?'

Samantha turned her horse. 'Come along,' she called to him. 'Jared and Lysle are at one of the marking grounds. Ride along with me; I'll show you.'

They loped across acres of rich, dark grass, their shadows running furiously on ahead, sometimes tall, sometimes short and thick. When Samantha finally slowed down to a walk Sheriff Wheaton could catch the pungent scent of burnt hair and hide. A little farther along he saw the dark little spindrift of smoke rising up around behind a long, low hillock which had a grove of shadowy scrub-oaks atop it.

Samantha stopped. 'Sheriff,' she said. 'They're around that hill working calves. You can't miss them.'

'I'm obliged,' John retorted, brushing his hatbrim to her.

'Sheriff; that doesn't make much sense. Ten thousand dollars because Lysle hit that man just once, for all the vicious talk he's been spreading about us. Tell me; what is he really trying to do?'

John Wheaton wasn't devious himself and rarely expected deviousness in others. He said, 'Samantha; as far as I know this minute, Whitsett's just after an easy ten thousand dollars. He's got a kinky-haired string-bean of a lawyer from San Francisco, or somewhere, back in town, waitin' to bring Jared and Lysle to court.'

'Ten dollars, Sheriff, yes, but ten *thousand* dollars?' Samantha shook her beautiful head of hair. 'It doesn't make sense. What is this Carleton Whitsett really after?'

John smiled. 'Maybe another punch in the nose,' he said, and lifted his reins to ride on around the hill. Samantha made no attempt to stop him, but she sat back there watching him go; he could feel her eyes on him until he passed alongside the spending curve of the hill and came finally into sight of the dusty, hot, sun-brightened marking ground where six or seven men, mostly on horseback, were holding and working a herd of at least three hundred anxious cows and calves.

He stopped, looked back, did not see Samantha, assumed she'd ridden off, and dismounted to walk on over to the fire. He began feeling foolish all over again, too. Ten thousand dollars for one punch in the nose!

Chapter Four

Jared's reaction wasn't quite the same as his sister's reaction had been. He and Lysle listened to all John Wheaton had to say, Jared accepted delivery of the legal paper, scanned it while behind him his men were sweatily and profanily dragging up calves to be worked at the fire, then, because the noise right there was loud and disturbing, he led Lysle and John off a little distance and there stepped into some shade to push back his hat, make a smoke, and to afterwards say, 'John; this is pretty silly. Where could he expect to come out ahead in a move like this? I don't even know the man, but I can tell you this just from his actions: He's a fool.'

Lysle said, 'I don't think so, Jared. I've never thought he was a fool. You go watch him some time, listen to him. He's as insincere and dishonest as they come; he's trying his damndest to start a fight for us with the townsmen or our neighbors, and he's offering to practically give away those pieces of land he bought. I don't take those actions as the mark of a fool. I take them as the sign Whitsett's out to get Big B involved in a real fight, so folks we've known a long time will shy clear of us. He's going to make the Burchams look as bad as he can—for whatever reason's in the back of his brain.'

John agreed with part of that. He knew some of the things Whitsett had done. 'Jared,' he exclaimed, 'you can get the judge to issue a restraining order; that'd make him desist.'

Jared was six feet tall and whipcord lean. He was a bachelor. His sister had once said Jared would never marry because he had a mistress—Big B. Now, he pulled off his roping gloves and thinly smiled at Sheriff Wheaton. 'I don't need a restraining order to keep this Whitsett from causing any more trouble. Forget it, John. Just forget all about it.'

'Wait a second,' warned the sheriff. 'Jared; you folks out here've had it mostly your way for a good many years now, but don't cause anythin' to happen to Whitsett like him disappearin'. That'd only make things worse around town and among the other ranches. Listen to me, Jared; folks are listenin' to this feller. I'm not sayin' they're pro or con, but they're listenin', and he's talkin' against Big B. Now if he was to up and drop out of sight . . . you understand?'

Jared understood. 'Nothing like that will happen to him, John, I promise you. But I don't want to appear as ridiculous as he's made himself look by also getting up a legal paper to quiet him.'

Wheaton was at the end of his rope. As a lawman he'd come out here to serve a paper and discuss Whitsett. He'd now done both. He'd even done more; he'd warned Burcham and Small against violence against the person of Carleton Whitsett. Within the scope of his official office there just wasn't much more he could do, so he said, 'Frank Arbuckle swears up and down this Whitsett's out to break you, Jared, and dismember Big B. That's pretty far-fetched if you ask me. But one thing Frank and Phil Chandler say isn't far-fetched, and that's simply that Whitsett's right clever. I'm watchin' him, though. The first wrong move an' I lock him up.' John nodded to lend his conclusive assertion solid substance, then turned to go across where his horse was, back closer to the branding fire.

Jared and Lysle solemnly watched him go. Jared Burcham had known John Wheaton since before Wheaton had been elected sheriff. Lysle had known him only since coming to the Gatling country, but with a man as uncomplicated as Wheaton was, that ordinarily was plenty long enough.

'Well,' Lysle said, as the two of them stood back in the oak-shade watching Sheriff Wheaton ride off, 'If honesty was always enough in this world, there'd go a feller who'd someday die rich and full of honors.'

Jared turned his lean, bronzed face, looking sardonic. 'Lysle; you're pretty disillusioned about men and life for a feller no older than you are.'

They went back to their work at the branding fire, John Wheaton rode back to Gatling, and the long day passed pleasantly along towards evening, and beyond evening, towards night. Sheriff Wheaton made a detour over west of town about two miles, to ride down alongside the southward stageroad where the liverybarn-owner had a house and a few acres. His visit had to do with an impounded saddlehorse someone had found wandering over east of town. The beast had saddle marks on it, and, when found, had even had sweat-out-lines where a saddle had very recently been on its back. But when found the horse was stripped down to his hide. He had a brand on his left shoulder no one locally had ever seen before, so the critter had been turned over to the liveryman who was, in this instance, pound-master for the town. The critter, in accordance with law, was impounded for seven days, duly advertised in the *Gatling Gazette* three times straight running, then was put up for sale to the highest bidder, and whatever he brought was divided between the poundmaster—for his care and keep while impounded—and the town.

It was an old process. Every cow-town from the Missouri to the Sacramento used it quite often; stray horses were not at all unusual. Why they were abandoned was anyone's guess, but in this instance, as the liveryman and John Wheaton concurred, an outlaw had probably ridden the beast from wherever he'd fled from, then had abandoned him, stolen a fresh horse, and had continued his flight. So far, though, no one had reported losing a horse.

But that wasn't unusual either, in a land where hundreds of loose horses roamed the ranges, waiting for their owners to round them up and get ready to use them. Perhaps in a month or two someone would come to indignantly report to John that one of his saddle animals had been stolen. By then, of course, catching the fugitive would be just about impossible.

But in this particular instance, John Wheaton was fortunate without even knowing it, for where he'd forked off to head down-country parallel to town, he'd left two dark shapes lying out there a mile from Gatling with their guns cocked and snugged back, waiting for him to ride into sight, and into bushwhacking range.

He spoke with the liveryman briefly about the estray, then headed right on up the southward stageroad directly into town. He left his horse at the liverybarn, sauntered over to his office, lit the lamp, tossed down his hat and dropped into his swivel chair, tired and hungry and uneasily disgruntled.

He didn't really believe Jared or Lysle would do anything to Carleton Whitsett; maybe, if Whitsett persisted in his troublesome ways, punch him in the nose again, but they wouldn't call him out with guns. They couldn't; Whitsett never appeared with a gun buckled around him.

But the more he turned over in his mind the implications, the less he liked any of this. That business of buying those worthless little parcels of land, then reselling them at cost just to bring newcomers into Cheyenne Valley. Or his inflammatory talk against Big B, when the Burchams had never done anything to him. And finally, the man himself. Carleton Whitsett just didn't belong; he was too smooth and handsome and confident. He always shaved. John ran a rough hand up the scratchy side of his own leathery face. He was always clean and presentable. John glanced at his own rumpled, sweat-stained attire. Finally, he stood up and yawned, making a promise he'd have a heart-to-heart talk with Whitsett the next day.

There wasn't too much he could say; Whitsett hadn't broken any laws, as John had told Frank Arbuckle. He could mouth off all he liked, providing he didn't actually come right out and make valid threats against the Burchams or Lysle Small. Still; as sheriff, John could warn Whitsett. Not just of the dangers inherent in his present course, but of the probable results if Big B got its dander up.

Someone lightly rapped on his roadside door. Wheaton blinked, stifled his yawn and called for whoever it was out there, to come on in.

The man who entered was Terry Wilson, barman up at Abner Folger's place. He had a sealed note for Sheriff Wheaton which he handed over looking annoyed, perhaps at having been used as someone's messenger-boy, stiffly nodded and departed.

John took the note across to his lamp, opened it and stood a long while gazing at it. Eventually he folded the paper, slipped it into his pocket and went across to scoop up his hat. He'd been sleepy when Terry Wilson had entered. Now he wasn't sleepy at all.

He blew out his lamp, opened the roadside door and looked both ways up and down the roadway. Gatling was quiet and dark except up at the northerly end of town where the saloons were, but even up there the noise was subdued in comparison to what it normally was on a Saturday night, say. But this was the middle of the week.

He stepped forth, crossed the empty, unlighted wide roadway, and strode along to the hotel where he and several of the town's other bachelor-residents kept rooms. Ab Folger's room was upstairs on the west side overlooking the roadway. When John rapped softly Ab called guardedly for him to walk on in. John did.

The room was dark. Abner was sitting over by the open window, a bulky silhouette in a candy-striped shirt and lavender sleeve-garters. He was smoking a cigar.

'I got your note,' John said. 'What's the big mystery? Why don't you light your cussed lamp?'

'Pull up a chair over here,' said the bar owner, twisting to watch the sheriff make his way gingerly across the cluttered room. 'Sometimes I like sittin' here lookin' out into the night in darkness.'

Wheaton carried up a chair, sat down, peered down into the dark and empty roadway, raised his eyes to gaze westerly over the building roofs out towards Burcham's range, and finally settled back. 'What's on your mind?' he asked.

'Murder,' growled the massively thick-set man seated next to him, without turning his head or removing the thick cigar he had clamped in his teeth. 'Yours, I think.'

Sheriff Wheaton continued to study his friend's heavy profile a moment before he said, 'Anybody I know?' Then smiled saturninely.

Folger lowered the cigar and finally turned his head. He wasn't smiling at all. 'John; tonight those two gunfighters who've been hangin' around town met Carleton Whitsett out back o' the saloon. I just happened to go into the storeroom to get some bottles for the bar. The window's open; it's always open this time o' year. I heard men talkin' up against the wall out there. I looked out and recognized those two, and Whitsett. He'd hired them for something; I got there too late to hear that part of it, but he handed each of them a wad of money. Then they sauntered off. I took the bottles out to Terry at the bar an' went around front to have a smoke—at least I figured no one'd think it looked odd, me bein' out there watchin' the tie-rack while I had myself a stogie.'

'Their horses were out there, Ab?'

'Yeah. They came around, climbed aboard and rode at a slow walk down in front of the jailhouse. They stopped there for a moment or two, but the place was dark. Then they rode on down to the liverybarn an' one of 'em went in to talk for a few seconds with the hostler, then they both turned off headin' westerly out through town towards the Burcham range.'

John leaned back with an oddly heavy sensation behind his belt. 'I see,' he murmured.

Folger said, 'I went down an' asked the nighthawk what they'd said to him. John; they asked which way you'd ridden when you'd left town earlier.'

Wheaton leaned back in his chair. 'I'm right obliged to you,' he said. 'Anything else, Ab?'

'One more thing. I was worried, so I took my pistol an' walked out through town too.'

'But you never found them,' said John Wheaton.

Folger nodded his massive head up and down. 'I don't know what I'd have done if I had found them, John. All the same, when I saw 'em stop out front of the jailhouse first, I had a notion they were lookin' for you. What the hostler said clinched it for me. Now; I been sittin' up here holdin' my breath ever since I sent Terry out lookin' for you with that note to come up here to m'room as soon as you got the note.' Folger leaned forward. For the first time John Wheaton saw the carbine and the long-barreled rifle leaning beside him against the dark wall next to the window.

John looked at his old friend. He started to speak, checked himself and blew out a big, ragged sigh instead. 'Pretty sorry night for it,' he commented. 'Not enough moonlight.'

Folger said, 'Hmph! If I've got those two snakes sized up right they wouldn't need any moonlight. All they'd need would be Whitsett's cash in their pockets. They'd get it done, one way or another—and John—if not tonight, then tomorrow, or tomorrow night. But at least we're warned, an' I been sittin' here thinkin' that's about two-thirds of any battle; knowin' in advance when the attack's likely to come.'

Wheaton said, 'We, Ab? Listen to me; this isn't your—.'

'See these guns beside, me?' growled the baby-faced, massive saloon owner. 'John; if I'd heard a gunshot *anywhere* out there tonight, which is why I been sittin' by this damned open window in the dark, *anywhere at all,* believe me when those two'd come driftin' back into town up or down the road, I'd have cut them down one at a time from up here in this dark window and left 'em lie. They'd know where the bullets came from, but they'd be dead, so no one else would know. In other words, John, what's sauce for the goose is sauce for the gander.'

Sheriff Wheaton raised both booted feet, propped them on the windowsill and said softly, 'But why? I don't understand it, Ab. Why me?'

Folger's answer wasn't very enlightening. 'I don't know. I don't care. I don't want Whitsett nor those two wolves of his in my saloon again under any circumstances. I aim to tell them that, too, the very next time I see them.'

Chapter Five

It took a little doing for John to talk Ab out of his fierce truculence, but he did it by reasoning out loud that if Folger tipped his hand and let Whitsett know he'd overheard anything, had seen all that Ab had really seen, then Whitsett wouldn't only turn crafty, he'd also turn against Abner too. His parting comment to the saloon owner was: 'Act like you've always acted, Ab. I'll look out for myself, now that I know I've got someone gunning for me. But unless we do it this way, Whitsett's going to know we suspect something, and right now I don't want that. I want to know *why* he's gunning for me, first; after I get that nailed down, if you still want to buy in, why then I'll deputize you, an' the pair of us'll take them on.'

Folger assented, not graciously at all, because he'd had a bad night of it and was still tense and overwrought, but he did assent, so John went along to his own room and wearily turned in. He'd missed his supper, as he'd known would be the case, he hadn't accomplished much by seeing Jared and Lysle, which he'd also known would be the case, and for all that, he'd very nearly ridden into a bushwhack set up by Carleton Whitsett.

He knew exactly where Fate had intervened too; out there on Big B range where he'd decided to ride on down to the liverybarn owner's place and discuss that public sale they'd be holding on that estray they'd impounded. He owed Ab Folger his gratitude; Ab would have avenged him without any question. But, as he drowsed off, he thought he also owed that damned impounded horse his life, and that was a little difficult to square up with his church-upbringing about the Divine Destiny of men. As far as he knew, angels didn't often take the shapes of estray, impounded nags.

The following day just short of noon John ran into Carleton Whitsett. The younger, better-looking man had a light bandage over the bridge of his nose, and it irked John no end to privately admit it, but even that bandage gave Whitsett a dashing, heroic appearance.

John had been leaving his office when Whitsett approached down the north plankwalk and called to him. John stepped out and waited, his face wiped clear of any expression at all.

'I understand you saw my attorney yesterday,' said Whitsett, then engagingly smiled. 'He left town last night on the last stage southbound. That should please you, Sheriff.'

'Why should it?' asked Wheaton bluntly. 'That feller meant less to me than the time o' day, Mister Whitsett. I told him what I thought—that you were makin' a laughin' stock out of yourself around here, with that suit over a punch in the nose.'

'I know. He told me all that. He also told me you said

he might get the next punch in the nose.'

'That's right, Mister Whitsett. And he might have, too, if he'd hung around,' said John, and went on to state that he'd served notice upon Jared Burcham he and Lysle and Samantha were being sued. Whitsett listened, pleasantly nodding his head, but when John was finished he stopped smiling.

'You don't like me, Sheriff,' he said softly. 'I'll live through it. All I ask is that you run your business and let me run mine.'

'Depends,' stated John, fighting down his irritation. 'Depends on what your business is, Mister Whitsett. I'll tell you this much; you go on talkin' against Big B and the next time it might not just be a poke in the nose.'

'Whose side would you be on, Sheriff?'

That time John's temper slipped a little. 'On the *law's* side,' he said sharply. 'That might be a good side for you to get on too, Mister Whitsett.'

'I haven't done a thing illegal, Sheriff. Not one—'

'Mister Whitsett,' exclaimed John Wheaton in a thin tone of voice, 'a feller doesn't always have to do illegal things. Doin' *unethical* things can lead up to illegal things. It can get folks bad hurt sometimes. I'll give you a little warning; leave off tryin' to stir up trouble against the Burchams. I don't know what your reason is an' I don't give a damn what it is, either. You're just one man. You keep this up and you'll be the star player at your own funeral. That's my warning.'

Whitsett's liquid-soft eyes lingered on Sheriff

Wheaton for a moment before the younger man broadly smiled and inclined his head in a mocking little bow. 'I'll keep your warning in mind,' he told John. 'All I ask in return is that you bear in mind that you're here to protect folks. That means me, whether you like me or not. I happen to know that Lysle Small is out to kill me.'

Sheriff Wheaton was surprised at first, by this announcement, then he turned quickly skeptical and suspicious. 'That's a strong thing to say about anyone, Mister Whitsett. I want to know where you picked up that information.'

But the younger man only continued to smile, stepped around John Wheaton and went sauntering on down in the direction of the liverybarn.

John thought of rushing after him, but he didn't do it. Instead he turned and went ambling thoughtfully over towards the general store. He was low on tobacco.

Phil Chandler was having a cup of coffee back by the iron stove at the dingy rear of the store when Sheriff Wheaton entered. Two clerks were working with customers so John stepped around, helped himself to a sack of tobacco, dropped a five-cent-piece on the counter and sauntered back where Arbuckle reached for another cup and filled it. As Wheaton came up Arbuckle held out the cup, saying, 'What's this about Whitsett suing Jared?'

John accepted the cup, nodded over at old Phil, and recounted what he knew of the lawsuit. Phil chuckled and slapped a skinny thigh. Frank, who was less susceptible to sudden amusement, frowned at the sheriff. 'Is that a fact?' he growled. 'Well; you know what'll happen to Whitsett? Folks'll laugh him out of the country.'

'Wish I was sure of that,' muttered John, sipping the coffee. 'Frank; if you wanted to land a man in a peck of serious trouble, what would you do?'

'What d'you mean—what would I do? I'd take down my pistols an' go—'

'No, no, no. Dammit, Frank. Think *modern,*' snapped John Wheaton, and Arbuckle's face screwed up into an angry and outraged expression. 'Think like this: You'd first tell folks he'd maybe threatened your life. Then you'd come pantin' into town on a sweaty horse an' show a bullethole or two in your coat. You'd swear up an' down that you was chased and shot at by this feller. You'd have him put under a peace bond so's he couldn't come anywhere near you. *That's* how folks do it nowadays, Frank. Then there's another way—you'd get someone knocked off. Maybe a sheriff. An' you'd have witnesses who saw this feller you want to land in hot water, say they saw the actual killing.'

Phil Chandler's shrewd old faded eyes were no longer the slightest bit amused. He and Frank Arbuckle were watching John very closely, very intently. Somewhere along the line they'd picked up just enough inference to believe, now, that John wasn't just making conversation.

When Wheaton finished, the saddle maker lifted his coffee cup, noisily drank, lowered the cup and said,

'John; for that part about killin' the sheriff—you got anyone particular in mind? Because yestiddy I got a good close look at those two unwashed gunfighters who've been hangin' around up at the *Antlers*, an' let me tell you somethin' from the sum an substance of one hell of a long lifetime: They're killers. They're not here to work as cowboys. Their kind just don't take to that kind of sweaty labor.'

Frank Arbuckle was less devious in stating his opinion. 'Whitsett,' he exclaimed in a suppressed voice which was charged with emotion. 'Whitsett's going to make his move, John. Otherwise, why the gunfighters; why all this pussyfootin' around? I told you a month back, he should be rid out of town on a rail.'

John nodded and finished his coffee and plucked forth the fresh sack of Bull Durham to roll a smoke. 'I was just talking,' he told them. 'Just shootin' fish in a rainbarrel, as the saying goes. I don't know a damned bit of this to be true.' He lit up, shot a hard look at his friends, then said, 'And neither do either one of you. So don't get to hatchin' any meanness towards Whitsett or those two gunmen. Take my word for it; I've got both eyes wide open.'

He left Phil and Frank, returned to the roadway and saw Jared Burcham and Lysle Small walking their horses down into town from the northerly stageroad. They didn't come down as far as the general store, but instead turned in up at Ab's place, tied up and walked on inside. Wheaton sighed, tossed away his cigarette and went walking up towards the *Antlers*. He didn't

45

expect any trouble although he knew Carleton Whitsett was inside, up there. He always was this time of day. In fact, since arriving in town, he'd more or less made the *Antlers Saloon* his business and social headquarters.

When John walked through the roadside doors he saw Ab behind his bar. That was unusual; Ab had stopped tending bar several years earlier. He hired a day man and a night man. But to John, the reason was clear enough. He sauntered on up to the bar where Ab met his mild expression of interest with an impassive face. Over at that shadowy corner table Ab and the sheriff played their evening game of cards sat three men: Carleton Whitsett, Jared Burcham, and Lysle Small. They were talking. That is, Jared was talking, and from the expression on his face John could guess that Jared was laying down a little Burcham law to Whitsett. Lysle turned his head, saw John watching, and turned back again without even nodding.

'Nothing'll come of it,' muttered Ab, polishing the same glass he'd been polishing for five minutes now. 'I've got the old shotgun under the counter here, if anything does bust.'

'It won't bust,' agreed John. 'How about a beer?'

Ab stopped rubbing the glass to peer at his old friend. 'Kind of early in the day isn't it?' he asked.

John nodded. 'Kind of a special day too.'

Ab brought back the beer. There were only those three men over at the corner table, Folger and Wheaton, in the saloon. Later, just before Whitsett arose, stepped around the table and walked out of the place, a bewhiskered big burly freighter stamped in, settled himself at the bar and called for whiskey. He was on his second glass of the stuff when Jared and Lysle came over to the bar, signaled to Ab for beer, then turned their solemn glances upon Sheriff Wheaton.

Jared said, 'No threats were made, John. Just a little talk.'

'About his lawsuit?' Wheaton inquired, and Jared shrugged.

'That too. He said he'd dropped the lawsuit.' The beer came, Jared and Lysle picked up their glasses, drank, then Jared said, setting the glass aside, 'This was Lysle's idea. For my part I'd have seen him in court— or hell—before I'd have talked to him. But it turned out to be a fair idea. He said he bore Lysle no particular ill will for that bust in the beak.'

Wheaton sniffed. 'No more ill will anyway, than a rattler bears the roadrunner who bites off his tail.'

Lysle's grave glance kindled with slow warmth; he obviously felt as Sheriff Wheaton felt on this particular score. Then Jared said, 'He's hard to figure out, John. If he's up to all I've heard he is, I don't see why he was so agreeable to my face just now.'

'You reckon it's because you wear a gun, Jared?' asked John Wheaton dryly, 'or because his nose is gettin' kind of sensitive? Well; whatever the reason, I'm glad he's simmered down.'

Lysle fixed Wheaton with a pale stare and said, 'Do you really believe that, Sheriff?'

John's reply was candid. 'No I don't. But you can't

arrest a man for his thoughts, Lysle. That's the trouble with the law. You can't land with all four feet on anyone, until a crime's been committed.'

'Sometimes,' murmured Small, 'that's too late, isn't it?'

John nodded, finished his beer and dug for a coin. Jared beat him to it; he paid for all their drinks, then he and Lysle walked on out into brilliant sunshine.

Ab Folger came along, scooped up the coins and darkly said, 'John; run Whitsett out of the county.'

'On what charge, Ab?'

Folger's baby-blue large eyes puckered up and glinted. In a half snort, half whisper he said, 'You know damned well what charge! For layin' that ambush for you last night; that's what charge!'

Wheaton gazed sardonically at his old friend for a moment, then he said, 'Ab; have you seen either of those gunmen around town today?'

Abner shook his head. 'I haven't been lookin' for them,' he replied. 'I've been in here all morning.'

'I looked for them, Ab. I even went down to the liverybarn lookin' for their horses. They're gone. The horses and the gunmen.'

'What of it? They'll be back. They're up to some meanness somewhere, sure as God made green grass.'

Wheaton didn't deny that possibility, but as he told Ab, he couldn't, under the law, chouse Carleton Whitsett out of town, let alone out of the entire county, without exposing Abner to very real danger for what he'd seen the night before. 'Unless,' he concluded, 'I

48

can pick up those two bushwhackers on the sly, take them into the backroom of the jailhouse and persuade them to talk. I need their statements that Whitsett set up a bushwhack. Otherwise, I've got nothing at all to use in running him out of the country.'

'Law!' snarled Ab, holding his voice down with a great effort. 'What the hell kind of law is that, that let's folks lay ambushes, then can't touch 'em? I tell you, John, the old-time law was a heap better. Take my word for that!'

John thought old time Wyoming law was better too; the trouble was, he'd taken an oath to hold up the new-fangled law. He departed from the saloon thinking some private thoughts.

Chapter Six

It was past suppertime. John and Abner were at their table playing pinochle when four dusty strangers came stamping into the saloon. From his position over in the shadows, with his back to the wall, John Wheaton commanded an excellent view of the entire saloon. There were perhaps ten or fifteen drinkers and card-players here and there throughout the big room when those four burly, hard-eyed strangers stalked in. Here and there a head turned, an eyebrow lifted. Those four were rangeriders, by their dress and general appearance, but they didn't act the part.

They shot quick, close looks all around the room.

When they spotted the badge on John Wheaton's shirt-front, they clustered a moment at the bar, then one of them stepped back, turned, and sauntered over to John's table.

He was a man in his early forties, heavy-shouldered, thick-muscled, with the granite jaw and scarred brows of a fighter. When he halted, Ab looked up a little irritably. He was losing for a change. The burly man met Ab's annoyed look, letting Ab's displeasure roll off him like water off a duck's back.

'Friend,' the dusty, travel-stained man said, facing John. 'I take it you're the sheriff hereabouts.'

John nodded. With a badge as shiny as a spur rowel on the front of him it'd have been a little difficult denying he was the sheriff.

'Well,' growled the burly man, fishing into a shirt pocket, 'me'n my pardners over yonder along the bar are lookin' for a man who's supposed to be hereabouts, who's wanted for murder up in Montana.'

Ab Folger, for the first time, showed interest. He hoisted his chair around and tilted his head to glance from the stranger over to the other three hard-eyed men lined up along his bar. When he looked back at the nearby stranger again he minutely examined his clothing. Finally he said, 'Mister; if I'm wrong I apologize in advance, but I get the impression you're a bounty hunter.'

The hard-eyed man took that like he evidently took just about everything else, without showing resentment or malice. 'Your impression,' he said evenly, 'is plumb correct, friend.'

John Wheaton put down his cards, pushed back his chair and gazed in a bemused way at the burly man. 'You got a description?' he asked. The bounty hunter didn't bother answering. He fished out the crumpled, limp paper he'd been digging for, spread it out very carefully atop the table, and looked quickly at Abner Folger when the saloon owner took one good look, then gasped.

'You know him?' asked the bounty hunter.

Ab didn't answer. He gripped both arms of his chair staring straight at John Wheaton. John had more control. He looked, looked again, then picked up the wanted poster, leaned back to catch more lamplight, and finally tossed the paper back to the bounty hunter.

'Where'd you pick that up?' John asked. But the bounty hunter, after Ab's sudden loud gasp, and his subsequent look of horror and pure astonishment, didn't answer right off. He instead folded his wanted poster, put it back into his pocket and gazed from John to Ab, and back again.

'I got it,' he answered, finally. 'Where or how ain't too important, is it, Sheriff? The man's wanted in Montana for murder. There's four thousand bounty on him. I got three friends doin' a little manhuntin' with me this spring an' summer. That figures out at an even one thousand dollars each. There's not enough to cut you or your friend here, in. But I'm right satisfied this feller's around Gatlin' somewhere, so we'll find him.'

The bounty hunter started to turn back towards the

bar. Sheriff Wheaton said, 'Just a minute, mister. You don't make any citizen's arrest in my bailiwick.'

'Under the law, Sheriff,' stated the bounty hunter, turning a little bleak towards Wheaton. 'We got the right to—.'

'Don't tell me the law, mister,' snapped John. 'You've got the right to make a citizen's arrest only providing you can't secure the proper offices of a duly elected or appointed peace officer. You *can* secure 'em. I'm sheriff here and I'm plumb available any time you want to try an' arrest that man.'

The bounty hunter shifted weight, settled upon one thick leg, hooked both thumbs in his shell-belt and said, 'We'll commence our hunt come sunup, Sheriff. We got a system worked out for this kind of work. It works right well.' The burly man lifted long lips away from his teeth in a macabre smile. 'It works right well. If you want to come along, fine. It's your county, like you just said. We'll be leavin' out o' the liverybarn come sunup.'

The bounty hunter walked back over to his companions and the four of them immediately hunched in close to speak back and forth in low growls. Abner watched that for a moment, then yanked his chair around and looked straight over at John.

'That was Lysle Small on their wanted poster,' he said. 'John; I've heard Lysle mention bein' up in Montana.'

Wheaton kept studying those four hard, rugged looking individuals over along the bar as he said,

'Yeah, I know. I've heard him mention Montana too. But hell, I've been in Montana. I reckon two-thirds of the men ridin' range in Cheyenne Valley been in Montana a time or two in their lives. That's not what's botherin' me, Ab. You heard that stranger say he an' his playmates had a workable system for this bounty hunting business of theirs, didn't you?'

'Yeah.'

'I'll tell you what he meant. He knows now you and I recognized that face on the wanted poster. He's not going to wait until sunup any more than I am. He's going to leave a couple of his friends here to keep an eye on us, and the other pair are goin' to start circulatin' around through town showin' folks that picture of Lysle, and askin' where they can find him.'

Abner got the drift of John's thinking and leaned with his massive arms atop the card table, his thick shoulders hunched forward. 'They'll head for Big B,' he said. 'The first man they stop'll tell them where they can find Lysle.'

John smiled and leaned on the table also, his eyes steel-bright. 'Now Ab, you're going to get up and go over and tell your barman to fetch us a couple of drinks, and as you're walkin' back here with him you're going to order him to slip out the back way, take your horse from the shed back there, and ride like the wind to Big B, tell Jared what's going on, and have Jared come into town with Lysle, and every armed rider he's got on the place. You got all that?'

Abner nodded. Over at the bar two of the bounty

hunters straightened back off the bar as though they meant to turn and walk out of the saloon. John said, '*Now,* Ab. Get moving.' Then he pushed back off the table, waited for those two strangers to turn away from the bar, and hailed them. 'You two fellers; I'd like a word with you.' He beckoned.

Abner arose and sauntered over to the bar. Those two burly, hard-faced strangers paused to glance back at their friends who were still at the bar, but who were now watching Sheriff Wheaton.

John said, 'All four of you, then. Come on over here.'

The bounty hunter who had showed John and Abner that crumpled wanted poster shrugged, jerked his head at the two men who'd been in the act of leaving, and ambled over to the table. John pointed to chairs. All four men sat. John looked at the only one of those four he'd spoken to before.

'Four thousand dollars is a lot of money,' he said.

Instantly the spokesman for those four began wagging his head. 'I told you, Sheriff, it's just enough for us fellers. We're not cuttin' anyone in.'

'Suppose,' said John, holding the full attention of those four, 'that I fixed it so's you boys wouldn't get that fugitive. Now I'm not sayin' I'd do that, you understand, but I *could* do it.'

The spokesman for the bounty hunters placed a thick, callused hand atop the table and softly drummed, all the while making his private appraisal of John Wheaton. Finally, he said, 'Sheriff; I'll slice a couple hundred off my stack—when we collect—but that's all we're goin' to do. Take my word for that.'

Abner came to the table without his barman. He had a bottle and six glasses in his hands which he put down and pushed at the bitter-faced men. Then he proceeded to pour.

'Three hundred,' murmured John, looking the strangers over one at a time, wearing a sly little smile. 'What's three hundred out of four thousand, boys? My way, you'll come out on top. Without my help, you're goin' out of this town a lot poorer than when you rode into it.' One of the bounty hunters started to say something. The spokesman silenced him with a slashing gesture of one hand. He glared hard at John.

'You guarantee anythin'?' he asked.

Wheaton shook his head. 'Not a damned thing, boys. I'll only promise not to get in your way. That's all, and if you're any good at your trade, that should be enough.'

The bounty hunter looked around at his friends, his face dark and stormy. 'Lousy two-bit cow-town law,' he snarled. 'You fellers want to peel off three hundred for this leech?'

One of the men reached for the shot glass Abner had filled, and drawled in the soft accents of southwest Texas, 'Hell, Chuck; like the man says, what's three hundred out'n four thousand? The fugitive's here, you said that yourself. We won't need this lawman, but we sure might need his official standin' to get this fugitive out of this feller's town. Sure. I'm for chuckin' the three hundred his way.' The Texan downed his whiskey, made a face, and pushed the shotglass away as though to arise from the table.

The others were also agreeable for roughly the same reasons, and said so, which left their spokesman no alternative. But he didn't give in gracefully. He slapped the table, spilling some whiskey, and jack-knifed up out of his chair. 'All right,' he growled at Sheriff Wheaton. 'You get your three hundred—*after* we get our man, an' *after* we get him back to Montana an' collect the reward.'

John held out a hand. 'Let me have another look at that poster,' he asked, took the paper, spread it out and studied it for a long time. Ab, looking over his shoulder, read and reread the poster, backed off to go over where customers were clamoring for bar service, and walked off shaking his head.

'You know him, don't you?' asked the burly bounty hunter of Sheriff Wheaton.

John folded the paper slowly and held it out. 'Sure I know him, mister. I'll give you a hint where you can find him, too. Right after you tell me where you got that poster.'

'Took it off a tree,' said the bounty hunter, shoving the poster into his pocket again. 'Seen a couple of fellers hangin' 'em up about forty miles north o' here.'

'So you just figured to hit Gatling,' murmured John. 'Mister; you boys are real optimists. How'd you know he wasn't down in Mexico by this time?'

'No problem there,' volunteered another of the man-hunters. 'We run onto a fancy-dan ridin' a flashy chestnut horse on our way south and showed him the picture. He did the same thing that barman did; he looked like he'd seed a ghost.'

John leaned far back ranging a sardonic look around at the four of them. 'So you wrung it out of him too, about where he'd seen this feller on the poster, and he said right here in Gatling.'

The manhunter nodded and turned, going back to the bar with his companions, where Abner was waiting, a limp apron tucked into his waistband, ready to serve them.

John arose, considered the whiskey glass nearest him which hadn't been touched, reached for it, tipped back and let the fiery liquor burn straight down. It made him shudder. He then strolled over to the door and passed out into the night. Right behind him came one of the manhunters. When John looked around, the stranger wolfishly grinned at him.

'Just in case,' the man murmured softly. 'Nothin' personal, Sheriff; just in case you had some notion of ridin' out to warn this fugitive. You know how it goes in a strange town.'

John said gravely, 'Sure,' then fell to making a smoke, and afterwards asked the manhunter if he had a match. As he was lighting up the other three came out, looked around, called their friend, and went down towards the liverybarn, speaking back and forth in low and guarded tones.

John remained up where he was, in front of the *Antlers Saloon*, leaning upon the front wall in dark shadows, smoking and watching—and waiting.

It wasn't much of a wait. When Ab came bull-like through his roadway doors John called softly to him. Ab hastened over. There was a suspicious bulge under Ab's apron now.

'Down yonder,' murmured the lawman, exhaling gray smoke. 'Walkin' down to get their horses before they start askin' questions. Did your night man get off all right?'

Abner nodded vigorously. 'And you stalled them long enough almost for him to leg it out there. By the time they get someone to identify that picture, then get directions on how to reach Big B, Jared an' Lysle and their Texans'll be all set up and ready to come on into town. I hope to hell they meet those four on the trail!'

'I don't,' sighed John Wheaton. 'Inquests take a lot of time and waste taxpayer's money.' He flipped away his cigarette and blew out a big sigh. 'This is beginning to make sense to me,' he said, but when Ab asked what he meant by that, Sheriff Wheaton just shook his head and kept watching those four men growing smaller down through the darker parts of town, as they approached the liverybarn.

Later, he straightened up off the saloon front wall and went ambling down to his office.

It took no particular genius to understand why he hadn't been able to locate those two gunfighters today. They'd been out putting up those wanted posters. Nor was it difficult to imagine who the fancy-dan was who'd acted out all that surprise when those four manhunters had showed him the likeness of Lysle Small on those fake wanted posters. The two had been those same men who'd tried to ambush him the night before, and the fancy-dan had been Carleton Whitsett.

What really worried John Wheaton now, though, was that other manhunters might also find those posters and come riding into Cheyenne Valley. For across each poster in bold black letters were the words: WANTED—DEAD OR ALIVE!

Chapter Seven

When every advantage except raw, brute force, is on one side in a defugalty it can be expected that raw, brute force will fail.

That was why Sheriff Wheaton took out his clasp-knife and calmly went to work paring his fingernails, cocked back in his swivel-chair at the jailhouse-office. Raw, brute force, multiplied four times, was by this time on its way out to Big B. Also by this time, he was confident, Jared and Lysle had been routed out of bed with the warning. Brute force was going to be in the saddle most of the night—for nothing. Even granting there just might be a meeting out there, as one faction headed northwest towards Big B, and the other faction headed southeast, towards town, it wouldn't be much of a confrontation in John Wheaton's estimation. Big B's ten Texans would inspire an awful lot of respect in four bounty hunters.

He finished with his fingernails, took out his gun and cleaned, oiled, and rubbed it down, holstered it and took out his watch. Not enough time had passed yet for Jared to be leading his crew into Gatling. He went to the roadside door and gazed up and down. There were lights at the liverybarn southward and more lights northward up where the town's saloons were, but there were no lights between, where the stores and offices of Gatling's retail establishments were.

He considered checking the liverybarn to see whether Whitsett had returned yet, and to also ascertain whether or not Whitsett rode a chestnut horse. He decided against it, stepped back inside and idly flicked through the sheaf of wanted posters piled on a shelf above his desk. He didn't expect to find anything there on Whitsett, and he didn't. For that matter he didn't even find anything on those two bushwhackers Whitsett had either hired here in town or had imported, but that didn't particularly surprise him either. The printing and distributing of wanted posters was pretty much of a haphazard business.

It was after twelve o'clock when Ab Folger came along and barged on in. He'd closed up the *Antlers*, he said, right at midnight; there wasn't much business left by that time anyway. 'Weeknights begin losin' their steam around ten,' he confided. 'By midnight I'm standin' around losing money.' Ab was wearing his coat. He unbuttoned it and sank down upon a little bench over near the cellblock door. There was a full cartridge belt around his middle and a six-gun in its russet holster on his hip. His smooth, round face with its china-blue eyes looked as boyish and incongruously innocent as ever, except for the faint droop at the outer edges of his mouth and the cold, total lack of warmth up around his eyes. 'You got it figured yet?' he inquired, while they sat and waited.

John told him what he thought. 'Whitsett's behind it.'

'That don't surprise me none, John. Only you got to hand it to him; he's smart.'

'Clever fits better,' muttered John. 'We can likely save Lysle's neck, but first thing in the morning I got to find out where Whitsett had those fake posters printed, and how many he had those two gunfighters of his nail up in the back country. The next thing I got to do is—.'

'Nail Whitsett to a wall,' growled Ab. 'I'll even help you pull his teeth, if you like.'

'Not Whitsett right off,' corrected the sheriff. 'Those two hired forty-fives of his. Whitsett doesn't pack a gun. At least not a visible one. But those men he either imported or hired here in town after Lysle hit him, not only *do* carry guns, but they'll use 'em. That's why I want to prevent. And after that—.'

The roadside door opened and Terry Wilson, Folger's night barman came in looking haggard and sore. 'They're comin',' he said, running a sleeve across his soiled lower face.

Ab left his bench. John got up also. They started forward. The bartender stepped aside, spied the water bucket with its dipper hanging suspended from a nail, and headed over to get himself a drink. As he did this he said, 'I met 'em on my way back. I eluded 'em, but they cut around an' followed me back into town. Damned if I know how they recognized me.'

John slowly came about. 'The bounty hunters?' he softly asked, and when Terry Wilson nodded, gulping down water, John and Ab exchanged a look. 'I thought you meant Big B,' Wheaton said.

Wilson turned his head. 'No. I meant them four brush-poppers. I was half way back from Big B when they showed up. I skirted wide and rode hard. They saw me and swung right around. They'll be here in a few minutes. I wasn't leadin' by more'n a mile when I hit town.'

John's shoulders slumped. He thought a moment then said, 'Did you see Jared and Lysle?'

Wilson nodded, wiping water off his chin. 'Routed 'em out, told them what I was supposed to tell them, then cut on back for town. Mister Burcham said for me not to wait; that I should get on back an' report to you that he understood and would come right on in, with his crew.'

Outside in the darkness several shod-horses trotted loudly down the deserted roadway, turned in at the roadway tie-rack outside, and stopped. John listened briefly, stepped to his wall-rack, took down a sawed-off shotgun, returned to his desk and settled himself on one corner of it, his left leg several inches off the floor, his scattergun pointed straight at the closed roadside door, and his thumb on one of the weapon's twin hammers.

Wilson hastily put aside the dipper and stepped back. Ab Folger swept aside his coat, drew his six-gun and sat back down on his bench with the forty-five tilted and aimed in the same direction. Also, with his thumb on the knurled hammer. When the door was kicked violently inwards, both men cocked their weapons. Those two little harsh sounds were unmistakable. Four angry-looking men pushing aggressively in out of the balmy night, stopped dead in their tracks, half through the doorway.

'Terry,' said Sheriff Wheaton coldly. 'Disarm them!'

The bartender moved reluctantly to obey. Thus far, the bounty hunters hadn't gotten a chance to say a word. They rolled their eyes from left to right, from that tipped-up cocked forty-five less than fifteen feet away, to the even closer lethal barrels of John Wheaton's riot-gun. That hard-faced, heavy-jawed man who'd been their spokesman earlier, put a kindling glare upon the sheriff. 'We should've known,' he growled. 'We never should've showed you the poster.'

'That,' contradicted Sheriff Wheaton, 'is the only *right* thing you did, mister. It kept all four of you from being buried here. That's not an authentic poster. I don't know who printed it but I'll find that out too. I can tell you for a fact, though, that those things were deliberately nailed up so that a man named Whitsett—the fancy-dan you met—could get strangers to kill Lysle Small.'

All four of the manhunters stared straight at John Wheaton, unmindful of Terry Wilson passing back and forth collecting their guns. Ab Folger said, 'Boys; if you'd found Lysle Small, you'd have found yourself facing an even dozen guns. Chances are you'd have been salted down, too.'

John Wheaton gestured, when Terry Wilson was stepping clear with the guns. 'Go over there and sit down on that wall-bench,' ordered the lawman. 'You're goin' to meet Lysle Small. You're also going to get a chance to see I'm not bluffing. He's on his way to town right now—with his boss and ten more rangemen.'

The bounty hunters crossed over, sank down, looked perplexedly around at one another, then settled back facing the sheriff again. Finally, as the astonishment wore off, their spokesman got red in the face with slow wrath.

'Those two who was nailin' up the posters,' he asked. 'They worked for this feller who wants Small killed?'

John nodded. 'Pair of two-bit gunmen who arrived in town a week or such a matter after Carleton Whitsett got knocked down in a local saloon by Lysle Small.'

'You mean this Whitsett feller wants Small killed just because Small knocked him down?'

John didn't answer that. The explanation wasn't that simple, he didn't feel inclined to fully explain, and besides, he could hear a party of men riding slowly southward down the empty roadway, outside. He eased down the hammer of his shotgun, placed the thing behind him on his desktop and stood up. While the others silently watched, he crossed to the door, opened it, and called softly to someone outside at his hitchrack.

'Jared; no danger. I've got the manhunters disarmed in here.'

Twelve bronzed men walked into the office, nearly filling it. Lysle Small was beside Jared Burcham. The ten rangy Texans, all armed and ready, fanned out left and right behind those two. For perhaps ten seconds the standing, armed men, and the seated, unarmed bounty hunters, traded hard looks. John Wheaton was content for all this to happen and said nothing until he saw the uneasiness beginning to appear among the bounty hunters. Then he said, 'Well, boys; I promised you a look at Lysle Small. That's him, right there in front of you.'

Jared turned, looking waspish. 'What's this all about?' he quietly demanded. John explained, starting with the first meeting he'd had with those four men over there on his wall-bench, and concluding with what he was careful to tell them all was strictly his own private theory of how and why it had happened this way.

Lysle shook his head when Wheaton had finished, saying, 'I've been tellin' you, Jared, right along, Whitsett's no fool.'

Burcham's brows dropped down into a dark look. He shot a critical gaze around at the manhunters. 'How does it feel,' he asked them, 'being used?' Then, before they could have answered, assuming that any of them would have, he said, 'Four thousand dollars is a lot of money. Suppose I was to make you a *real* offer of that much for—?'

'That's enough,' snapped Sheriff Wheaton, before

Burcham could finish. 'Jared; we'll have none of that. I'm trying to *prevent* a massacre, not sponsor one.' He plucked a large iron key off a nail and strode across to his cellblock door. 'You four step up,' he growled. 'You're goin' to be guests of the town of Gatling for a few days.'

The spokesman for those manhunters got swiftly to his feet looking defiant. 'We didn't do nothin',' he exclaimed. 'Maybe we come close, Sheriff, but we still didn't do it. You can't lock us up for what we almost—.'

'You're wrong, mister,' snapped Wheaton, swinging open his cellblock door and jerking his head. 'I'm lockin' you four up for the *intent* to commit a crime. I can't hold you because you didn't actually *commit* it. But by the Lord Harry's ghost don't buck me, boys, because I'm perfectly within my rights to hold you twenty-four hours on suspicion, and if I have to I'll deputize every man in this room to back me up. Now get up an' come on over here!'

The bounty hunters got to their feet waiting to see what their leader would do. He didn't have any choice at all, and this was very obvious. Jared Burcham, Lysle Small, and behind them, ten yeasty Texans, all of whom had less use for bounty hunters than they had for rattlesnakes, were waiting to take an active part in forcibly locking those four men up. With a savage curse the head manhunter stamped across the room.

John locked them all in the same strap-steel cage in his backroom, returned to the office and closed his cellblock door. As he crossed over to hang the iron key back upon its nail Jared said, 'John; we could've stayed at the ranch and run them off.'

Wheaton's answer to that caused another long, thoughtful silence throughout the room. 'Sure you could've, Jared. But last night Whitsett set up an ambush for me when I came back from Big B. I'm not sure what his reason was, but I've got an idea he was goin' to produce witnesses to claim they saw either you or Lysle kill me.'

The standing rangemen looked astonished. Their eyes followed Wheaton to his desk where he sank down and swiveled the chair around towards them. He was faintly smiling up at them, but without much warmth or mirth in his eyes.

'But that's only part of it. Those four we just locked up were the first ones to find those fake posters. There'll be others. Maybe tomorrow or the next day. Or maybe they'll slip in during the night. If Lysle's on Big B range, or even in the bunkhouse out there, he's goin' to become a target for every money-hungry bounty hunter in the country. Whitsett's clever, like Ab says, so we got to team up an' be a little smarter. Lysle; I'm goin' to lock you up right here in my jailhouse and Jared, you're goin' to leave me five men by day, an' five by night, to stand guard. That's the only way I know to keep Lysle alive until we can pin Mister Whitsett's ears to the wall.'

Jared Burcham looked at his rangeboss, then stepped over beside Ab Folger, who had holstered his six-gun, and sank down. He was nonplussed. So were the other Big B men in the little office. Lysle went to the water bucket, got a drink, and squared around gazing down at John Wheaton.

'I don't understand all this,' he murmured in the silence. 'What can he do by getting me salted away, John? I'm only the rangeboss at Big B.'

Ab Folger spoke up for the first time since the Big B men had arrived. He said, 'Lysle; if John's thinkin' is right, why then the way I see it, you're only a minor thorn in Whitsett's side, but as soon as he's got you out of the way he'll move against Jared too.'

Burcham looked up, his expression a twisted grimace. 'The man's crazy,' he said. 'He's got to be. We've never done anything to him. I've only talked to him once, John. He's got to be out of his mind.'

Wheaton shook his head. 'It's not altogether you, Jared, if I've got Whitsett figured right. Look how he dresses; how he acts. He's a man with nothing, whose sole ambition in life is to *be* someone. He hates you with a violent passion because of what you are and what you have. His kind's not new on earth, Jared. Believe me; his kind's damned common. He'd kill you if he dared, without even knowing you, because of his consuming envy. It's taken me a while to see that, but I sure see it now.'

Chapter Eight

Lysle consented to being locked up in the cell adjoining his would-be assassins and Jared Burcham left five of his men on guard inside the jailhouse with the promise to John Wheaton that the other five would relieve those original five guards sometime during the following day. Then Jared left, riding back out of town with his head down and his shoulders slumped. As Ab said, mightily stretching and biting back a big yawn, there wasn't anything quite as helpless as a man who's being venomously attacked without any real or valid reason for it.

Ab took Terry Wilson and departed. John meant to follow along close afterwards; it was late and he was tired. It had been a long day and a longer night. First though, he showed his Big B rangemen through the jailhouse; showed them his barred and locked back-alley doorway, his gun-rack, his ammunition drawer, and finally he tossed his personal set of keys on the table along with a greasy deck of cards. 'Don't let anyone in unless you know him right well, and unless only one man enters at a time.'

He left them with the night as still and benign as any late springtime night could be. There were series of blue-white stars scattered at random across the curving, high heavens, and a silence as deep and as endless as all Eternity, stretching over the world. Cheyenne Valley was passing through another of its insular, untroubled nights. Or so it seemed, anyway, as Sheriff Wheaton trudged on over to the hotel, pushed on inside and started clumping up the stairs to his room. He opened his door and a thunderous explosion accompanied by a blinding rush of orange-white light slammed straight at him from inside, over by the fire-escape window on the room's far side.

He felt a stunning breathlessness as he was hurled back out into the hallway, across it, and struck the wall hard with hips and shoulders. It was a numbing totally unexpected occurrence. There was no sense of actual physical pain right away, only that leaden, appalled sensation of having been shot.

He knew he should grab for his gun but the order couldn't for some reason be transmitted to his right hand and arm. He also knew he was sitting against the hallway opposite his own open door in plain sight of that assassin, and should at least roll away, and he couldn't do that either.

He didn't lose consciousness, but it was very hard to breathe. He saw something shadowy moving from right to left back there against the distant wall of his room. He felt his nerves and muscles functioning as though he were totally detached from them. He heard the deafening roar of a six-gun and flinched when his right elbow was slammed backwards into the wall under fierce impact. Then a sense of wonderful warmth stole up through him making him turn drowsy and loose and easy.

The passage of time was telescoped; he never afterwards had a clear notion at all of how long he lay out there between being shot and between trying to twist his head away from several sharp slaps on his left cheek, but when he looked up Ab Folger, the hotel proprietor, and Doctor Alfred Bean were kneeling around him looking rumpled and frightened. It was Al Bean who was lightly slapping his cheeks, so he made a hard effort to swear, and heard the words come out thick and gusty. Doc Bean stopped slapping and reared back on his knees looking relieved.

Al held something out to the doctor, saying, 'Look at that, Al. You ever see anything like that before?'

The physician said he hadn't, and only a lifelong bone-head deserved that kind of luck. Then he arose, stamped the kinks out of his legs and said, 'Come on, Ab, give me a hand. We'll pack him inside and put him on his bed.' They dragooned the hotelman into helping too, then, after he was aware of being stretched out on his own mattress, they ran the hotelman out despite his loud and persistent protests, closed the door and stood briefly gazing down at him. He still clung to consciousness with a doggedness which was characteristic. Ab went over by the fire-escape window and leaned there gazing out into the cooling late night for a long while. The physician peeled back John's shirt, probed here and there, always managing with diabolical efficiency to touch a sore place, then dragged up a chair, sat down upon it and studied the sheriff's face.

'Can you hear me, John?' he asked, and when

Wheaton nodded, rolling his head sideways to see what Ab was doing, the doctor held out something where John could see it. I've heard it said all my life these things on the front of a man's shirt were targets.' He turned the badge over and over with his fingers. It was bent and twisted completely out of shape. 'But this is the first time I ever saw that literally demonstrated. His bullet hit your badge head-on. It's a plain miracle, John, at that range, the slug didn't push this piece of plated steel right through into your lungs. I can't understand—unless because the thing was loosely pinned on—why that didn't happen.'

Sheriff Wheaton raised a hand, took his badge and gazed at it. The center was dented so deeply, the metal had been so punched out of shape, that nested in the middle of it was the piece of flattened lead from his ambusher's gun, obliterating the lettering completely, except for the first and last letters.

His chest was sore and for a full half hour he didn't dare take down a deep breath, but the numbness departed, his nerves and muscles resumed functioning, and eventually he shakily raised up, rolled his feet over the edge of the bed and sat there gazing around. Ab had lighted his table-lamp. He saw, over near the window where Folger was still looking out, where a man had smoked several brown-paper cigarettes where he'd crouched near his escape-route, waiting. He also saw scuffmarks from run-over boots. Finally, he said, 'Damn!' and stood up. Doctor Bean cautioned him.

'It's late, John. Lie down and rest for what's left of

the night. By morning you'll be sore and stiff, but you'll feel a lot better.'

Wheaton ignored the physician and looked over at Folger. Ab grimaced, strolled over and said, 'Well; it could've been worse, John. He could've hit two inches to the right, in which case the country'd be lookin' for a replacement come sunup.'

John said, 'What were you lookin' at, down there, Ab?'

Folger pursed his lips a moment in thought, then said, 'Can you walk?'

'Hell yes I can walk,' muttered Wheaton. 'I wasn't shot in the *legs!*'

Ab raised his hand, crooked a finger and crossed to the doorway. He stepped out into the lighted hallway, waiting. He wasn't smiling, but there was a look of hard, tough satisfaction in his baby-blue eyes, which impelled both the wobbly lawman and the medical doctor along behind him. He led them downstairs into the deserted, faint-lighted little shabby lobby and on outside and around into a side-alley. There, Ab stopped below the fire-escape near a bundle of lumpy rags. It was dark and hushed in this little passageway. Objects were difficult to make out. Wheaton placed his right hand on his holstered six-gun and peered around. The physician stepped around him, went ahead fifteen feet and halted, looking down.

Ab reached with his left foot, dug into that pile of loose rags and flipped the body over onto its back. John moved up and stared.

'Know him?' Folger quietly asked.

John knew him. So did Ab Folger. He was one of that pair of gunfighters Carleton Whitsett had sent out posting those counterfeit dead-or-alive posters. John eased down upon one knee gingerly, being careful how he breathed, and bent to look for the wound. Al Bean struck a match. The gunfighter hadn't fallen to his death, as John first thought, he had a round, black bullethole through his body from back to front, high up and dead-center.

Bean sniffed and killed his little sputtering light. 'Dead before he hit the ground, boys; I wonder who got him?'

John looked up at Folger. 'You, Ab?'

Folger blinked, stood a moment, then wordlessly bent down, lifted out the sheriff's six-gun, opened the gate and revolved the cylinder until he came to the expended casing, and wordlessly handed the gun back to its owner. John looked and frowned, then shook his head as he put away his gun. He had no immediate recollection of having fired that shot. Later, he recalled his right elbow slamming into the hall wall, and hearing a gun go off, but except for his moral certainty that he'd fired as the bushwhacker was outlined in the fire-escape window, he never actually remembered shooting at the man.

Doc Bean helped John back to his feet. The town around them was dark and hushed. The only two sets of lights came from down at the liverybarn, where lamps burnt all night on each side of the roadway entrance, and over at the jailhouse where Jared Burcham's Texans were keeping their armed vigil.

John put a hand gingerly to his hurting chest. 'There were two of them,' he said, in a nearly normal voice. 'The other one'll be around somewhere.'

Doc Bean was skeptical. 'Not tonight he won't, Sheriff. If he'd been close enough to let you have it, by now he'd have done so. All the same, you'd better get back upstairs. I'll have this man taken to my place for embalming first thing in the morning, and if you like, I'll come round to your room right after that and bandage that cut you've got.'

Ab smiled, looking straight at the lawman. 'No need, Doc,' he murmured. 'He'll walk over under his own power for the bandagin'.' Then, putting a hand upon Wheaton's shoulder, Ab said, 'Come along, John; it just happens I got a fresh bottle of gen-u-wine Irish whiskey hidden in my room. That's the best medicine there is for a feller who's just looked Death straight in the eye, then walked away to tell of it.'

Doctor Bean didn't dissent from the saloonman's prognosis. He simply gave the sheriff a light, friendly, slap, and walked back out of the little narrow alleyway.

John had to stop twice as he and Ab climbed the steps inside the hotel, to catch his breath. The pain was becoming sharp and insistent, finally, as the last of the shock departed. At the upstairs landing the hotelman was waiting, his coat and trousers on this time, looking mystified and anxious.

'You sure you ought to be out o' bed?' he asked the

lawman. 'Where did he shoot you, Sheriff?'

John fished in a pocket, brought forth his smashed badge, dropped it into the hotelman's palm without a word, and followed Folger down to Ab's room. There, while Folger dug for that secreted special bottle of whiskey, John speculated. What he came up with sounded far-fetched even to him, but right then it was the best he could do.

'Ab,' he said, watching Folger working strenuously at the bottle-cap, 'the other night I couldn't for the life of me figure out much of a reason why Whitsett tried to have me bushwhacked. The best I came up with was what I told Jared and Lysle tonight— because Whitsett would produce witnesses, maybe those two hired guns of his, to swear under oath in court they saw Lysle do it. But now I'm beginning to look at this some different.'

Ab said, 'Sure,' and handed the opened bottle to John. 'Take two big swallows of that. If it doesn't kill you it's bound to cure you.'

John took one swallow. Ab hadn't misrepresented; that whiskey was as smooth as sour cream. He took the second swallow. Immediately, he felt the dull, rich warmth moving out through his body with a wonderful mellowness. Even the pain in his upper body seemed relieved, at least temporarily. He smiled and handed back the bottle.

'You were sayin'?' murmured Folger.

'I got a different notion of all this now, Ab. Whitsett needs me out of the way because if there's no law around when the manhunters who see his counterfeit wanted posters start drifting into town, there won't be much to stop them from getting Lysle Small.'

Ab tilted back his head, let the whiskey flow down, sighed and smacked his lips as he approvingly gazed at the bottle a moment, then handed it back to the sheriff. Finally he said, 'John; you got to change your tactics. This quit bein' a one-man crusade about an hour ago. Whitsett's got one more gunman that we know of. Those damned posters of his'll bring in maybe a dozen more. On top of that, there's the sore-heads around who agree with all those silly lies he's been peddling around town against Big B. All in all, Carl Whitsett's got all the ingredients he needs to start a full-scale war against Big B.'

John took one more long pull on the bottle, set it aside, and raised his hand to gingerly probe his injured chest once more. He sat for a while in thought, and meanwhile, off across the high-arching yonder heavens, visible through Folger's roadside window, the sky began paling. Began turning that watery, blurry, very soft-steel shade of wet blue which preceded the soft pinks and reds which presaged dawn.

The night was gone, somehow, although for John Wheaton it didn't seem that so many hours could have passed. Shock very often carries with it that sensation of hanging in time and space. He shook his head; the whiskey made him feel nearly normal again. He said, 'Ab; you've been wanting to buy in. I'm goin' to let you do it. But not openly. I want Carleton Whitsett. I've got to get him and that other gunman of his before sun-down. The gunfighter won't show his face around town, I'm pretty sure, but Whitsett might. His kind's always cocky. By now he may suspect how much we know, but once he told me I couldn't lock him up; that I didn't have evidence against him, or something to that effect, so maybe he'll show up today. You keep your eyes peeled. Pass the word to Phil Chandler and Frank Arbuckle to do the same. I've got to nail him before those bounty hunters who see his fake posters start riding in.'

Ab nodded, beaming broad approval. 'I'll pass the word,' he agreed. 'We'll be sly about it, John. What'll you be up to?'

'I'm goin' to get Jared, maybe a couple of his boys, and search this damned countryside for five miles in all directions. I can't wait for Whitsett, I've got to *find* him!'

John went back to his own room to wash up, change his torn shirt, reload his forty-five and briefly rest before going out into the fresh new day.

Chapter Nine

The ride out to Big B wasn't especially painful, but it wasn't comfortable either, for John Wheaton. Mainly, though, he was tired. The pain was there, under his shirt where a sullen, bluish swelling had risen, and where the broken skin was irritated by his shirt. But by this time, the morning after, he felt pretty much as Doctor Bean had felt; a miracle had saved his life. A man could feel physical pain and still be grateful because he *could* feel it. Dead men felt nothing.

He reached the headquarters-ranch well short of noon but with a good warmth loosening the muscles of his back. Jared was there. So were his riders; they were idling here and there, obviously under orders not to leave the ranch. Two of them were cleaning a hollowed-out-log watering trough. One was out front of the barn where he'd strung out some chain-harness, which he was indifferently cleaning with old rags and saddlesoap. Two more were out back in a round corral, working with a wild horse. At least the beast acted wild. Dust hung golden in the air back there; the cowboys hooted and laughed, and occasionally swore.

Jared waited for Wheaton to ride on over and gingerly dismount in front of the two-storied, white-painted, very impressive big main-house. As John stepped down, and as Jared started down off his pillared porch towards him, Samantha came around the side of the house with her heavy hair caught back at the base of her head and held down by a little green ribbon. She looked cool and calm and capable, as she always seemed to be. Sheriff Wheaton touched his hat to her and she smiled over at him.

'Jared,' he said. 'I've got to find Whitsett, an' I've got to do it today.' He explained about the attempt on his life, then also explained why he had to have Whitsett in custody. 'If that devil has his way he'll stay out of sight an' Lysle'll get dragged out of my jailhouse by those damned bounty hunters who'll be driftin' in. I've got to have Whitsett, to put a stop to all that.'

The cowboy over at the barn tie-rack, made a long, low whistle, which appeared to be some pre-arranged signal, and pointed out into the dazzling sunlight northward. John and Jared turned. Two riders were coming in at a careful walk. They were lanky, faded men with bedrolls behind their cantles, and Winchester saddle-guns slung forward under their saddle fenders, pushed up a notch so that the carbines could be instantly drawn.

Wheaton sighed. 'They don't waste any time.'

Jared nodded, looked around and waved his left arm. Immediately his Texans faded from sight down by the barn. All this, evidently, was also by pre-arrangement. 'You're on your toes' murmured John Wheaton, finishing his turn so that he was facing those oncoming horsemen. Jared kept right on stonily regarding the strangers too, when he answered that.

'A forewarned man, John, is a forearmed man. We've been ready since last night.'

The strangers rode right on up, gazed from Jared to John and back to Jared again. One of them said in a low drawl, ' 'Mornin', gents. We're lookin' for a feller by the name o' Lysle Small. Folks told us over on the east range beyond Gatlin' he works over here.'

John said, 'Boys; forget it. In the first place Lysle's in legal custody. In the second place, those wanted posters are counterfeit. And in the third place, the man who told you where to find Lysle Small is wanted by the law himself.'

The cowboys sat and gazed at John Wheaton, at Jared, at Samantha over near the edge of the long porch, then loosened in their saddles. The other one said, 'Feller; you got all the answers. Couldn't be you're out here lookin' for him yourself, could it?'

Jared spoke up, his voice hostile. 'You're talkin' to the sheriff of the county, boys, John Wheaton. Everything he told you is the truth right down the line. Now, if you'll turn and look back over by my barn, you'll see five excellent reasons for heading right back up north where you came from, without even stoppin' for a smoke on the way.'

The five Big B Texans were over there with carbines in their hands, ranged along the barn-front looking drowsy and languid, and very lethal. Both those man-hunters turned, looked, then faced forward again. One of them shook his head morosely. He wordlessly fished in a pocket, brought out a carefully folded piece of paper and let it fall to the dusty earth. 'Never really fancied myself a manhunter anyway,' he muttered, and turned his horse.

As those two were walking stolidly back out of the yard Jared said, looking at them, 'Those are the first.'

'Not the last though,' exclaimed John Wheaton. 'An' unless I'm sure guessin' wrong, the next pair will be more than just footloose cowboys lookin' for an easy four thousand. That kind of a reward-offer brings in the top-notch killers and hunters.' He drifted his glance over where the rangeriders were still standing, also watching the departing bounty hunters. 'Well, Jared; do we make a search, just the pair of us, or do we weaken our forces by takin' along a couple of your men?'

Jared didn't hesitate over his answer. 'I'd feel a sight better, John, if we left the men to guard Lysle, and just the pair of us went looking.'

Samantha walked over and asked if John had visited the jailhouse before he'd left town. He had, and told her that he had. He also told her Lysle was one of the worst prisoners he'd ever had, and she smiled about that. Then he and Jared went down to the barn where Jared sent his five Texans into town to replace the other five, and after that Jared saddled up to join John in a big sweep of the countryside.

They both knew every foot of the land they were covering. They also knew every rider and cowman they might meet over east of town, but only twice did they see riders and the first time evidently that rider saw them first and had no wish to talk with them, for he appeared up over a low hill about two miles northeast of Gatling, looked down where they were loping along, swung, and dropped from sight down the far side of his knoll. They skirted around over there looking for him, but the man had made good time; by the time they reached where he'd been, he'd faded from sight northward, the direction his tracks pointed.

The second time they were more fortunate. The rangeman they encountered was a small rancher over near the distant foothills. The man's name was

Wilburn; years back he'd ridden for Big B, so Jared knew him quite well. Wilburn told them he was on his way to town to pick up some supplies and ammunition. The wolves, he said, were particularly bad in the hills this springtime. He'd already shot seven at his calving grounds, and every few nights more of them came down from the mountains to kill a calf or two.

John asked if Wilburn had seen any strangers around, and when he got a head-wag by way of answer to that question, he asked if Wilburn had seen a fancy-dan riding a handsome chestnut horse. That time, John struck pay-dirt. Wilburn pointed. 'See them slopes west o' the stage-road pass over towards Big B? Well, Sheriff, yestiddy I was doin' a little pot-hunting over there near a salt lick the elk and deer usually hang aroun', and I come right up onto this fancy-dan you're describin' with the patch over his beak, talkin' to a real pair o' hardcases. A tall one an' a short one. Gunmen, I'd say, from the looks of them. They never seen me, an' as soon as I saw them, I slipped back around into the hills an' got t'hell away from there.'

John and Jared gazed over where Wilburn had indicated. If Carleton Whitsett had met his two gunfighters up there the day before, there wasn't much chance of any of them still being there. John knew for a fact the smaller gunfighter wouldn't still be over there, because he was cooling out in Al Bean's woodshed down in town, waiting to be loaded full of formaldehyde before he was planted in Gatling's boot-hill boneyard.

Wilburn knew no more and rode on southward,

heading for town. Jared and John Wheaton turned back towards the northward country. Neither of them were hopeful, but as John said, they had to start their man-hunt somewhere.

They didn't reach the low hills until the sun was high above them. By then, too, the heat had built up. Jared knew of a waterhole and led out for it. They had to pass in and out of a number of random low hills, sometimes covered with brush, sometimes bald except for an occasional pine or oak tree. Then they hit fresh sign of horsemen.

'That'll be from yesterday,' pronounced Jared Bur-cham, stopping to lean down from his saddle for a closer inspection. 'It looks like two of them went southeastward.'

John nodded. 'That'd be the pair of gunfighters. I'm curious about where Whitsett went after that meeting.'

Jared straightened up, looked around, and said, 'It shouldn't be hard to find that out, John, if you want to back-track a mile or so up into the foothills.'

John was bone-dry. 'Any water up there?' he inquired, peering doubtfully towards the hills.

There wasn't, Jared said, and led out once more heading for the place where he knew there *was* water. It was near to one o'clock by then, the heat was at curling height, their animals were beginning to suffer, so John let his mount follow Jared's horse without directing the horse with his reins, and fell to thought-fully speculating about the plausibility of a hideout back up in those shadowy foothills. He'd felt confident earlier that the surviving gunfighter wouldn't show up in town again, although he didn't have that feeling about Whitsett. One was bold and blustery, the other was quiet and ferret-like, and secretive.

They came around the heavy haunch of a sturdy low hill, saw the green place up ahead where a grove of wild trees made deep shadows across a pool of sky-blue water, and rode right across a very fresh set of shod-horse marks without even noticing them, because they were gazing up ahead.

They weren't more than a thousand yards off and closing in, when the gunshot came out of those yonder trees, dropped John Wheaton's horse like the blow of a mighty sledgehammer, and sent John sprawling forward. The shot had come so entirely unexpectedly that Jared Burcham yanked back on his reins and for a space of three or four seconds, just sat up there looking round-eyed over where John's horse gave one quick convulsion, then turned loose all over, shot right through his head.

Then Jared left his saddle in a lunge, dragging out his Winchester as he fell. The second gunshot from those trees was just as accurate as the first one had been. It hit dead-center where Jared had been, but was not now.

John scampered on all fours to get behind his dead horse. There was no other cover within twenty yards in any direction. He flopped down, ducked his head and waited. Sure enough, the third bullet struck his dead horse with a hard, meaty sound. He wiggled along and peered out. Jared reared up, fired, levered and fired again, then he whipped upright and raced furiously for the protection of John's dead horse. He made it, but without much time to spare. Evidently his two shots had forced that assassin over there at the spring to duck down just long enough for Jared to reach safety.

The unseen man's next shot ploughed up a big cloud of grit and dust, which cascaded down behind the dead horse making Jared swear, and making John brush a soiled sleeve across his face.

Now, the invisible gunman over there fell silent. John threw a bullet over where he'd been firing from, just to make a test, then he flung around and said, 'Jared; watch out. He's moving. He'll go right or left in those damned trees to see around the horse.'

That surmise was correct. Jared was moving away when, from up ahead and far to the right very near the farthest extremity of his small oases, the gunman let fly one more time. The bullet tore the heel off Jared's left boot, wrenched his ankle violently and brought a suppressed groan and curse past Burcham's clenched teeth.

There was no doubt about it; whoever that man was over there, he was extremely deadly with his guns.

John removed his hat, lifted the dead horse's head with painstaking slowness, propped the thing up with his six-gun, then scooped out a place where he had about six inches beneath the horse's head and neck to peer slit-eyed from. He could see a partial stretch of the onward trees where the last shot had come from, but he could not be seen himself.

He waited, sweat from his recent exertions running into his eyes and darkening the armpits and yoke of his shirt. Jared got his twisted ankle out of sight and lay aside his guns as he curled low to get his boot off before the sprained ankle swelled too much. There wasn't a sound through this breathless interval.

John squinted his eyes nearly closed to keep out the salt-sweat, and kept watch. He didn't even turn to see how Jared was making it. It was a tense and painful vigil, but finally he saw faint movement up there in the foremost tier of trees. He dropped his chin into the dust, hunched around his carbine and took long aim. The movement came again; their attacker was stealthily coming down through the trees beside the pond to look out from a better point of vantage. He finally straightened up, one hand on a tree trunk, the other hand on his grounded carbine. That was when John fired.

The stranger over there was tight-wound. When the bullet struck he sprang straight into the air, emitted a choked-off cry, and fell, to roll out into bright sunlight without moving.

'Got him,' said the sheriff, pushed back, retreived his six-gun, raised up cautiously in case there were more than one of them over there, then stood up and walked forward.

He reached the assassin without incident, knelt to roll the man over, and turned as Jared hobbled up, using both their carbines as crutches.

'Know him?' Jared asked through clenched teeth.

'I know him,' John replied, arising. 'He's the other

member of Whitsett's pair of hired guns. I got the shorter one last night. Now, this one.'

'He had to have a horse around here somewhere,' growled Jared. 'You'll need it to get back, John. We'd better find the critter.'

Chapter Ten

They found the horse without much trouble. It was grazing back in the cool shade where green grass grew. It was a gaunt, tough animal, ugly in most ways but built for speed and stamina. Precisely the kind of horse a gunfighter would need. When John led the beast out of the trees, Jared was bathing his purple, badly swollen left ankle in the pond of cold water. He looked, started to speak, looked past the horse John was leading, and darkly scowled.

'He was a rustler too,' said Jared.

John hadn't even sought a brand on the gunman's horse, but now he turned and looked. There was a Big B on the beast's left shoulder. John said, 'I'll be damned,' and looked round-eyed over at Jared. 'I think I can trace our dead friend now.'

Jared was puzzled. 'By my stolen horse?' he asked.

'No, not exactly. But there's an impounded stray down at the liverybarn with a brand on it no one around here's ever seen before. That feller I shot over there was riding this horse of yours. My guess is that the impounded strange critter at the liverybarn was his. He abandoned it when he stole this one.'

Jared bent to examine his sprained ankle. 'Well; all he got was rawhide toughness, pretty fair speed, and an evil disposition, when he stole that critter. Lysle told me last week when the boys brought in part of our remuda, that danged horse was missing.'

John looked doubtfully at the purple, puffy ankle. 'Can you make it, Jared, or should I go on back to the ranch an' have 'em send back a wagon for you?'

'I'll make it,' replied the rancher. 'Just give me hand up into the saddle.' As John bent to obey, Jared said, 'We didn't even get a whiff of Whitsett, John.'

Wheaton wasn't concerned, right then, about that. He wanted to get Burcham home safely, then head on back into town to send some telegrams. He had a hunch the dead gunfighter was from Montana. He knew the brand on the impounded horse, so what he had to do now was send a descriptive telegram to the U.S. Marshal up at Butte, in Montana, requesting that verification be made through Montana's bureau of livestock identification. Not that identifying the dead gunfighter was likely to aid him find Carleton Whitsett, or, for that matter, prevent Whitsett's clever scheme of getting duped bounty hunters to do his dirty work for him. But on the other hand the more he knew of that dead man, the more it would satisfy him about his suspicions of those two hired killers.

He got Burcham across his saddle, tied Jared's boot to Burcham's saddle, got on the dead man's horse with the corpse lashed aft of the cantle, and started back down-country towards Big B's headquarters home-place.

They had to make haste slowly. Jared was gray around the lips from each jolt and bump on the long ride. All he said though, was that John had forgotten to tank up on water back up there. John's reply was succinct.

'Lost my thirst when I lost my horse.'

They got back to the home-place just before sun-down. The five Texans who'd spent the night in town were there, dozing around their bunkhouse until they saw that grisly procession of three men on two horses walk into the yard, then they came wide awake and rushed out to help their employer off his horse. John asked about the prisoner in town. The Texans said up until they'd departed, when their relief-riders had come in, nothing had happened. John told Jared to take care of that ankle, then turned and booted out the ugly Big B horse heading straight over the open range for town.

The men back there in the yard watched the lawman and his flopping passenger go, without a word passing among them. Dead men lashed behind sad-dles weren't uncommon in this raw and violent land, but flopping ones secured behind living men atop long-legged stolen horses weren't something they saw every day.

By the time Sheriff Wheaton reached Gatling, dusk was falling. He entered town from across the Cheyenne Valley range and jettisoned his burden out back of the doctor's place, then rode around front, knocked on the door and when Al Bean came out looking quizzical, Wheaton told him he'd left a corpse in Bean's backyard, and went back to his horse, mounted up and headed straight for the liverybarn, leaving Doctor Bean gaping after him.

There was no handsome chestnut horse stalled down at the barn. John told the hostler to turn the Big B horse into a stall and grain him, then he went out back and made one last study of the brand on that impounded critter before heading over for the telegraph office to dispatch his inquiry to Montana's U.S. Federal Marshal. After that he went to his jailhouse, got past the tough-faced Texan at the door, and asked how the prisoners were making out. One of the Big B men smiled and jerked a thumb over his shoulder. 'We fetched Lysle some o' the grub from the cafe an' he liked to had a fit.'

Wheaton went into the cell-room and at once those four bountyhunters started yelling at him. He waited until that little windstorm subsided, then, talking to Lysle Small, told what had happened up in the foothills earlier in the afternoon, and concluded by reciting his experience out at Big B with the second pair of down-at-the-heel-looking pair of amateur bounty hunters. Lysle was impressed; so were the four men in the adjoining cell who finally fell silent.

Lysle said, looking out at Sheriff Wheaton, 'What about Whitsett, John? Until that son of a gun's run down, this thing'll only get worse.'

John agreed with that, but said, 'As long as you're

safely under lock an' key—and with good guards—
Whitsett's about my only worry. I'll get him, Lysle.
Don't you fret about that.'

One of the bounty hunters in the adjoining cell said
dourly, 'Sheriff; ain't no one man livin' who can buck
a feller as smart as this here Whitsett's turnin' out to be.
Tell you what: Set us loose and we'll hunt him down
for nothing, and fetch him into town to you belly-down
across his saddle.'

John didn't even answer. He turned, went back out
into his office, then left the jailhouse building, bound
northward up to the *Antler Saloon.*

But that paid no dividends either. Ab had just
returned to his bar from checking with Frank Arbuckle
and Phil Chandler; none of them had seen hide nor hair
of Carleton Whitsett.

While John and Ab were talking, Terry Wilson, the
night bartender, came down to them at the far curve of
the bar and muttered under his breath. 'Take a look at
those three strangers up there at the far end o' the bar.
They just asked if I'd heard of a feller named Lysle
Small around town.'

Abner twisted and looked. So did John, but Wheaton
also sighed. Those three made five manhunters in one
day. He pushed off, sauntered up and leaned upon the
bar next to the rough looking strangers. 'You've got a
wanted poster,' he told them, not asking a single question. 'It says Lysle Small's wanted in Montana for
murder—four thousand dollars worth. Boys; it's a pure
fake. Small's not wanted as far as I know, but anyway,

I've got him locked up under armed guard across the road.'

The three rough rangemen owlishly stared at Sheriff Wheaton. One spoke up in a suspicious tone: 'Mister; if you're the sheriff hereabouts, how's it come you ain't got no badge hangin' on the front of you?'

Abner came along with a limp bar-rag to mop and re-mop the worn bartop in front of those strangers with one hand in sight, with the other hand down under his bar.

'The badge got busted,' said John amiably. 'Now head out. There's nothing here for you or your kind, at all.'

One of those rough men screwed up his face and laid a scarred, large fist atop the bar as though to snarl something at Sheriff Wheaton. Ab reached over and rapped the man on the knuckles, and when those three manhunters turned, Ab pushed the twelve-inch, big-bore barrels of his under-the-bar riot-gun straight up at them. Then Ab smiled.

'You call it,' he told the strangers. 'Spit or close the window, boys. Start blastin' or start ridin'.'

For ten seconds no one made a sound. The strangers moved their eyes from Ab's gun to his broad, smiling countenance, then down to the gun again. One of them sighed and gave his head a little shake. 'Pure unfriendly town,' he murmured. 'Pure unfriendly, bar-keep. We'll just ride on out.'

They walked across the saloon and glided out through those two louvred roadside doors. When they were gone, someone laughed aloud. Down the bar stood one of Jared Burcham's Texans from over at the jailhouse. When John scowled, the cowboy raised a defensive hand. 'Just come over for beer, Sheriff. Lysle's orders. Ab; six beers in a bucket.' The rangeman dropped a coin and grinned again. 'That was real neat,' he said to Sheriff Wheaton. 'Seems there's more o' them scum than a feller figures there are.'

'Four thousand dollars is a pile of money, too,' replied Wheaton. 'An' if you didn't already know it wasn't genuine, you'd probably be after it too.'

He left the saloon to stroll down towards Frank Arbuckle's general store but didn't quite make it. Doctor Bean caught up with him and breathlessly said, 'Thanks a lot, John. If this keeps up I'm goin' to put in a claim against the town for my embalming fluid.' He dug around in a coat pocket, brought out a squashed-flat piece of paper and held it out. 'Found this in the dead man's boot under the sock,' he said.

John carefully unfolded the paper. It was another wanted poster, but this time it had the dead man's likeness on it, along with a description of his crimes. He was wanted in Cut Bank, Montana, for murder. He was also wanted in Idaho for horse-stealing. The rewards totaled eighteen hundred dollars.

John said, 'Thanks, Al. I could've saved myself a silver dollar if I'd known about this earlier. I sent a telegram to—'

'Hey, Sheriff!' a man yelped from on down the

roadway, waving a yellow slip of paper aloft from his telegraph office.

John excused himself and sauntered on down to accept the reply to his wire. He read it, re-read it, then exchanged a long look with the telegrapher without either of them saying a word for a moment. Around them, night was fast settling over Gatling. Here and there a light sputtered on. Men and women were hastening homeward up and down the plankwalk.

'Be damned,' John said, finally. 'Come on; I've got to send another telegram.'

He and the telegrapher entered the latter's office. John emerged ten minutes later heading for the cafe, his expression long and pensive. The reply he'd received from the U.S. Marshal up in Montana hadn't only identified the brand on that impounded horse, it had also given a resumé of the man who'd stolen it, *and that man hadn't been the dead gunfighter at all!* He was named Carleton Whitsett, or at least the U.S. Marshal said that was one of his names, and he'd been last seen heading south after being hired by cattle interests to organize a range war in the Big Horn Basin. In that war seven men had lost their lives!

John's telegram back to the U.S. Marshal had asked for more particulars, saying he had Carleton Whitsett in his own territory, and that Whitsett was already responsible for two deaths—his own hired gunmen in both cases—and was now hiding somewhere in the Cheyenne Valley country. But that Sheriff Wheaton was under the impression that Carleton Whitsett was from San Francisco, not Montana.

Frank Arbuckle walked up. He too was on his way across to the cafe. 'What you dreamin' about?' he demanded of John. 'Or did that near-miss last night scramble your brains?'

'If it scrambled them,' breathed Sheriff Wheaton. 'I just got the low-down on Whitsett. And that *un*scrambled them.'

They went into the restaurant, took a table and signaled for their supper, which was never a matter of choice in Gatling; rather, when a customer sat down, he automatically became eligible for beef stew or lamb stew or deer-meat stew, or just plain vegetable stew, whichever happened to be on the stove, and the menu, for that night.

'No Whitsett, eh?' mumbled Frank, tucking a napkin into his collar.

John told him all that had happened this day. Frank listened, looking black in the face, and when the lawman finished he said, 'I told you weeks back, John. I told anybody who'd listen, Carleton Whitsett was a fraud an' a fake an' a troublemaker.'

Their supper came, also their coffee. Several men drifted in out of the settling night, mostly townsmen who, like John and Frank, were bachelors, and after nodding, strolled over to the counter where the service was quicker, if nothing else was any different. The last man to walk in was old Phil Chandler, the saddle and harness maker. He came across to the table, looked at both men and waited for one of them to ask him to be

96

seated. Frank did, and Phil dropped down, raising an arm so the restaurant's proprietor would see him, then he heaved a mighty sigh and said, 'By the way, I just saw one of your haulin' wagons come into town around back, Frank.'

Arbuckle nodded and grunted as he dug into his stew. 'It's the one that's been overdue all day. It's fetching in a load of hardware from beyond the valley. Funny thing about hardware; in the summer an' winter I don't move enough of it to pay the storage space out back in the warehouse. But in the springtime I can sell twice as much as I've got no matter how much of it there—.'

'And the driver was lookin' mighty peaked,' said Phil Chandler, breaking in as though Frank hadn't uttered a sound. 'Got a big bandage around his head and one arm in a sling.'

Frank's fork, halfway to his mouth, halted in mid-air. He and Sheriff Wheaton looked straight at the saddle maker. Chandler's stew came, he considered it without the least bit of enthusiasm, pushed back his chair and said, 'Well; what are we waitin' for? Your driver'll be over at Doc Bean's by now. Let's go.'

Chapter Eleven

Phil was right. Frank's wagoneer *was* over at Al Bean's dispensary getting properly patched up. When the sheriff and saddle maker walked in, along with the

97

driver's employer, the men raised a yeasty stare to the three of them.

'What happened?' Frank asked, his dark brows down and his eyes like ice-chips beneath them. 'You have an accident, Bent?'

The driver's arm was freshly slung from a black length of cloth and Doc Bean was snipping away some of his bushy black hair to examine the wound atop his head. Doc shot one sardonic look over at Arbuckle, then murmured, 'You might say he had an accident, Frank. A lead-poisoning accident. This is a bullet-crease or I never saw one.'

'Well?' demanded Frank, glaring at his driver.

In a stolid tone the man called Bent said, 'Mister Arbuckle; you ever been shot at five times an' hit twice? No? Well; when you have you'll want a slug of whiskey before you set down to write your memoirs.'

Frank got red in the face, 'Damn it all,' he stormed, but was cut off by Al Bean who stepped back, opened a cupboard, brought forth a bottle and handed it to Bent. 'On the house,' he said, and went back to cut away the man's black, coarse hair.

Bent drank deeply, corked the bottle and wiped away tears with his good hand. Then he began to get a little color back. 'Was comin' down across the valley on the stageroad,' he recounted, holding the liquor bottle firmly by its narrow neck, 'an' seen these riders. I figured they was Big B men. Didn't really pay too much attention, Mister Arbuckle, because I was a little weary from the long haul. Then they stopped out on the range

98

east o' the road for 'while, like maybe they was talkin' or somethin', an' right after that here they come.'

'How many?' asked John Wheaton.

'Seven, Sheriff. Six I never seen before an' that dude who was hangin' around town few weeks back just before I pulled out.'

Frank said in a velvety tone, 'You mean Carleton Whitsett, Bent; is that the dude you're talkin' about?'

'Mister Arbuckle, I never heard his name. Right good lookin' man about your height, with a little patch over the bridge o' his nose like maybe he'd cracked it, ridin' a—'

'Chestnut horse,' put in John Wheaton.

Bent nodded, winced, and after that didn't move his head again. 'Yeah; ridin' a big goodlookin' chestnut horse. Well; they swung out across the road an' fanned out to stop me. It was the way they done that. I've been stopped before. After all, like you know Mister Arbuckle, I been drivin' stages, freighters, one kind of rig or another twenty year'. When I see 'em fan out like a skirmish line I know it's trouble. It was a mite late, maybe, because they wasn't more'n few hundred feet ahead, but I reached down and yanked the carbine from its boot. That's when the nearest ones opened up. Boys; there was lead jumpin' all aroun' me. I felt the one go through my arm an' dropped the carbine to hang onto the lines. All that sudden commotion set the horses to fidgettin' like a hitch o' young colts.' Bent rolled his muddy eyes around. 'That's all I recollect until I come to with the sun dang near down. I had a headache to end all headaches, an' the blood had run down into my eyes. For a second there I was scairt pea-green; figured I'd been blinded. But when I sat up and wiped off, it was just this here crease over the top of my skull which split the hide a little, bleedin' like a stuck hog.'

'And the men?' asked Sheriff Wheaton.

Bent shrugged. 'Gone, Sheriff. So was my company purse, my own personal poke, and a case each of carbine an' six-gun ammunition, which was among the hardware goods I was fetchin' back t' town.'

For a long moment no one said anything. Each man digested all this in his own way. It was the physician, finishing up with Bent's head-wound, who finally said, 'Well, Frank; you got off lucky. A couple of boxes of ammunition and your money. It could've been the whole wagon and a dead driver.'

Arbuckle nodded. John Wheaton stepped across to a chair and dropped down. 'Bent,' he said, 'did you know any of those men except the fancy-dan who was leading them?'

'Like I told you, Sheriff, I never seen any of them before in my whole blessed life.' The driver paused, made a face as Doctor Bean hurt him, then said, 'But I can sure tell you this much, Sheriff: Them fellers sure knew their business. They stopped my wagon just like they'd have stopped a bullion coach. An' when they went for their guns, believe me Sheriff, they were gen-u-wine professionals.'

Phil Chandler was making a smoke, saying nothing and looking thoughtful. Doctor Bean growled at him not to light his cigarette in the dispensary, so Phil nodded, popped the thing between his lips and let it hang there, unlighted, while he said, 'John; he's got himself a little army now. Maybe he gave up on stampedin' some of the local boys into doin' *all* his dirty work for him. Or maybe things weren't movin' fast enough for him. But now he's on the warpath for sure. Two boxes of ammunition, seven men, and a daylight strike against one of Frank's wagons. In my day that'd have added up to a real war-party.'

John had nothing to say. He agreed, at least in substance, with the harness and saddle maker. He had an idea now why Carleton Whitsett hadn't returned to town. After what had happened in town last night—the killing of his hired assassin—he'd decided to not wait for bounty hunters to see his counterfeit wanted posters and hunt down Lysle Small, but had decided to hang back in the country where he'd had those posters nailed up, and recruit the men himself.

It was possible too, that by now he knew Lysle was locked up. After all, John had told five different men who'd also drifted into town to collect that bogus reward, he had Lysle in his jailhouse, and those five had ridden away knowing that.

But the problem wasn't so much the fact that Whitsett now had a band of seasoned killers riding for him; the problem was to discern—if possible—what Whitsett would do next.

John arose. Whitsett's warped hatred had, right from the start, been directed against big and rich and powerful Big B. With seven guns—and the element of surprise—he just might be able to attack the Burchams right in their own yard. It was the elimination of Jared, by one means or another, which had been Whitsett's dream right from the start. With that many guns—and a solemn promise of a cash reward if they'd help him— he just might make a direct drive on the headquarters-ranch now. He'd certainly be too smart to try and ride into Gatling with seven guns and get Lysle Small out of the jailhouse. The only thing left, then, was an attack upon Big B.

John's heart missed a beat. There wouldn't be ten Texans out there; there wouldn't be more than five of them, plus Jared, who was crippled now. And those five Texans would be lethargic from their previous night without any sleep!

'Frank,' he said. 'Go get Ab. 'You got any more of your men handy?'

Arbuckle looked perplexed. 'What men, John?'

'Drivers, damn it, or clerks; anyone we can make a posse out of. I need at least five men to head for Big B with.'

Even the physician looked surprised. 'Big B?' said Frank Arbuckle. 'You mean you think Whitsett'll raid Big B?'

'He's been tryin' to stir folks up into warrin' against the Burchams ever since he came here, hasn't he? Well; he didn't quite get that done before things started goin' sour for him, but he's sure got the means to make war on Jared now.'

Phil Chandler plucked the unlighted cigarette from between his lips and uttered a startled curse. The suggestion John Wheaton had just made struck him hard. It struck them all hard. Frank started for the door. So did John and Phil Chandler. Bent would have gotten down off the dispensary table and gone too, except that Doctor Bean held firmly to his shoulder and his one good arm. 'You've already done your share,' he admonished. 'You gave Sheriff Wheaton the clue to what this madman Whitsett's up to.'

'But I'd like one more crack at them devils for shootin' me,' stated the wagon-driver darkly.

'Not in the shape you're in,' persisted the physician. 'Anyway, they won't need you.'

Outside, the men split up. John hadn't asked old Phil Chandler to fetch his horse and guns for the reason that Phil was well past the age when men ought to fight. But evidently the old saddle and harness maker was oblivious of this, for he headed straight down for his shop, his skinny old long legs pumping up and down like pistons.

John hastened to the liverybarn, barked orders for Arbuckle's horse to be saddled, and went over to bring forth his own animal and start rigging it out. He'd just finished bridling and was laying on the double saddle-blanket when Ab Folger came trotting in breathlessly, with Frank and four other men, all toting their carbines, and a couple of them who'd evidently been getting ready for bed when they'd been routed out, also tucking in shirt-tails and carrying shell-belts as well.

The last man to show up was old Phil Chandler. But he was already mounted. He had his carbine balanced across his lap. When John saw him and paused at the saddling, old Phil called in to him.

'Well, come on, boys; if it's a fight they want we got to get a move to oblige 'em.'

Someone back behind John chuckled. He turned. Frank and Ab were back there with their horses, looking tickled. John didn't say anything. Neither did anyone else. They didn't take the time to admonish old Phil. Either that, or they just didn't have the heart to admonish the old man.

The nighthawk was helpful. He was also mightily curious but no one told him anything, so when the possemen got astride and went whipping around to head westerly out of Gatling into the starlit night, he went out to stand there watching them rush away, vigorously scratching his unkept hair.

They loped for two miles then slowed to blow their animals for one mile, then loped again. In this fashion they covered a lot of countryside before John slowed them, finally, and called for a halt. They were close enough now, he told them, to hear any fighting if there was any going on. None of them heard a thing. The night was well advanced, turning cool, totally quiet, and getting darker as the moon dropped away, lower and lower.

Phil summed up his thoughts about that heavy silence. 'It's either all over by now—or else it ain't started yet.'

John agreed with that in strong silence as he led them onward at a fast walk. For a moment, when they were within cannon-distance of the headquarters ranch, they got a brief scare. Up ahead a band of horses suddenly heard them coming, and exploded in all directions. One of Arbuckle's men swore and yanked out his six-gun, but old Phil guessed what that was up ahead, and said, 'Easy, boys, easy. Those aren't ridden horses; they're loose ones. Don't shoot; if there's anyone out here in the night with us you'll let 'em know we're comin'.'

Chandler was right. Ten minutes later, when they spotted some of those curious horses standing off a discreet distance looking at them and softly snorting, the man who'd gone for his gun leaned and said, 'Mister Chandler; you ever been an outlaw?'

Someone laughed. It sounded like burly Ab Folger. Old Phil snorted and looked down his nose at the man who'd asked that question. 'If I had been I'd have to be gettin' senile to admit it, wouldn't I, what with the sheriff ridin' right up here aside me, boy?'

That time the laughter ran all around, like a little ripple of distant water rushing over rocks. Even John and Frank smiled. 'Well,' stated the man who'd asked, 'seems to me you sure can call the shots on a manhunt like this. You was right about not wantin' any shots fired, an' you was right about them bein' loose horses up there.'

Old Phil's miffed look passed in the paleness. He said, 'Young feller; when I was your age a man didn't have to be no outlaw. All he had to be was out in a place like this with hostile warbonnets all aroun' him; he dang soon learnt what sounds were important an' which ones weren't—or else they held a wake for him back in town.'

That satisfied the younger man. No more was said until they came over a little rise which permitted them to see in all directions for as far as the darkness permitted. John halted, dropped his rein-hand and looked over at Frank and Ab and Phil. They looked straight back at him. Up ahead, although they couldn't make out the buildings, lay Big B's headquarters-ranch. If there'd been any trouble, even before they'd arrived out here, there'd be lights on down there. There wasn't a light anywhere. The atmosphere was drowsy and benign. No scent of gunsmoke, no echoes, no sights to show there'd been a fight.

John let his breath out in a long rush. 'Well; I'm glad to be wrong,' he told the others. 'Other times in my life I've come a-hellin' it on a mission like this, and found nothin' left but ashes and bodies.'

Phil Chandler slowly bobbed his head up and down. For old Phil, this was his last charge through the night with an armed party of men, and he seemed now to almost suspect that. He said softly, 'Amen, John, amen. I've seen places bigger'n Burcham's outfit scrubbed out right down to the watchdog. Burnt to the ground, butchered, hair lifted—nothin' left. I never begrudged losin' a night's sleep for any of it, but most of all when I seen 'em untouched, when I was scairt to take the first look.'

Frank and Ab were relieved too, but Ab suggested that they'd better ride on down and warn Jared anyway, then hit Samantha up for a pot of black coffee before they lit out back for town again.

John nodded, lifted his reins and eased his horse out over the last short mile. Up ahead a horse caught their scent and whistled shrilly. That was the only sound until they came into the yard. Then an armed man's rifle grating over a corral stringer stopped them in their tracks while John called out who they were.

Chapter Twelve

Jared was summoned. He came out pushing in his shirt-tail, his shell-belt loosely hung from one shoulder. When he saw the size of the party sitting their mounts out front in the cool night, he stopped to look, and raise an eyebrow.

'Trouble, John?' he inquired, gazing over where his sentinel stood, holding a carbine crossways up in front of his body.

Wheaton got down. So did all the others. Old Phil was last to alight; he was also the stiffest at it. 'No trouble,' exclaimed John. 'But Whitsett's got six gunmen riding with him now, Jared. I thought we ought to warn you about that.'

Jared looked at them all, then said, 'Takes this many men to warn me, John?' and shook his head. 'I've known you too long, Sheriff: Why the little army?'

'He hit one of my wagons,' explained Frank Arbuckle. 'Shot up the driver, and stole a couple of cases of ammunition, Jared. We sort of figured, if he was armed and ready for it, he just might hit Big B. After all, it's been Big B right from the start he's been dead-set against.'

Jared finished with his shirt-tail, buckled on his shell-belt, bent to lash the tie-down thongs of his six-gun holster, and gazed over at John Wheaton. 'That makes better sense,' he said, and afterwards straightened up again. 'I had a sentry out, John. If he'd come he wouldn't at least have hit us by surprise.'

Old Phil Chandler said, 'Mister Burcham; I've seen sentries killed with their own scalpin' knives, then propped up in plain sight with their rifles.'

Jared turned, considered the harness maker for a moment, and jerked his head towards the house where a light had come on. 'Let's go have a cup of java, men. Samantha's up now.' As he stepped back from the edge of the porch, Jared turned on his good leg, looking over towards his shadowy cowboy-sentinel. 'Go on back, Burl,' he said. 'Keep as good watch next time as you did this time.'

They entered the big house, doffed their hats and followed Jared on through into the huge combination dining-hall and kitchen. Samantha was there, as Jared had said, making a big graniteware-pot of hot java. Its good aroma filled the room. As Jared motioned for the men from town to be seated, he went over where someone, undoubtedly his sister, had placed one boot, and one felt slipper. He sat down, got his footgear on, and gazed around at the others, whom he hadn't really had a good view of, out there in the shank of the dwindling night. Of them all, Sheriff Wheaton looked most weary. He got up, hobbled out of the room for a moment, returned with a bottle of whiskey just as handsome Samantha was filling their cups, and laced each one, but put a double lacing in John Wheaton's cup. After that he sat down, felt for his tobacco sack, which he didn't find, accepted the makings from old Phil, and said, 'For your trouble, boys,' and raised his fortified black coffee in a salute.

It was pleasant in the big kitchen, sitting there under orange lampglow talking and relaxing, after that long ride and the tension which had ridden all the way out here with each of the men from town. Old Phil told them a couple of yarns of other rides like this one he'd been on, years back, when the results hadn't been nearly as gratifying. Otherwise, the talk skirted around the subject of Carleton Whitsett. It didn't follow any general pattern for the elemental reason that its subject, Carleton Whitsett, hadn't permitted it to, by his past actions, except in the one basic theme of his overwhelming envy and hatred of Big B.

Ab Folger theorized about that, and struck very close when he said, 'It takes all kinds to make a world. Whitsett's kind hates without reason and schemes without compromise. Why did he shoot up Frank's driver? With that many guns all he had to do was throw down and wait for Bent to toss out his gun. But Whitsett's crazy on this one subject of smashin' the Burchams. It doesn't make a whole lot o' sense to me, but I know one thing; if someone doesn't stop him directly, there's goin' to be blood get spilt.'

John finished his coffee, felt much better, and told them what he'd accidentally discovered through that telegram from Montana. 'He's a professional trouble-maker. Not a gunfighter; not himself, he'd hire all the gunmen he needed. He's the kind that organizes things; that lays out the dirty work and does the big talkin' to get folks stirred up. He's ten times as dangerous as a gunfighter. You can call a gunfighter out into the roadway and settle with him in a minute or two. Whit-sett's kind doesn't even carry a gun. At least he doesn't pack one where it shows. An' he tries to keep within the letter of the law. He's more dangerous than fifty gun-fighters.'

Phil Chandler yawned and shook his head at Samantha when she came over to refill his cup. The old man was gallant. He said, eyeing Samantha's strong beauty and heavy hair, 'Thirty years back, ma'm, I'd have sat right here drinkin' your coffee and thinkin' what a right beautiful woman you are, until I just sort of floated out of the place. But now all I can do is sit an' look, and admire. Coffee keeps me awake.' He smiled, got up, placed his chair back exactly as it had been at the big oilcloth-covered table, and winked at Samantha. 'I'll go outside an' have me a smoke. I'm right obliged for your hospitality, ma'm.'

Samantha smiled at the doughty old man, and

watched him saunter back out through the parlor towards the yonder front porch for his smoke. 'He reminds me of my father,' she softly said. 'In their day a man didn't smoke inside the house, he just naturally went out onto the veranda after supper.'

Jared chuckled, gazing at his sister. She was full dressed but her wealth of wavy hair hung softly past her shoulders. 'Ways change,' he told her lightly. 'So do men. In paw's day a man such as this Carl Whitsett wouldn't have lived this long.'

John stifled a yawn and leaned as though to arise, it was very late, he'd missed most of his rest the night before, and even that double-laced jolt of black coffee hadn't entirely alleviated his tiredness. He was about to stand up when the gunshot came, clear and sharp and loud-sounding in the tailrace of the long night. For a second he sat frozen, then he sprang up, his tiredness dropping away.

There was another gunshot, but that one sounded closer; out across Big B's night-darkened yard. Perhaps down where that sentry had been standing, in the general vicinity of the log barn and the corrals. They were all on their feet now, hands on their holstered guns. Jared swung and limped swiftly out through the parlor towards the front of the house. John passed him with thrusting strides, halting beside the ajar door to look out.

There was nothing to see, nothing to hear, but the bitter-acrid smell of burnt gunpowder was in the still outside night air. Over at the bunkhouse there was a solid, stomping sound, but no light and as yet no sign of life. Someone over there had jumped out of bed into his boots.

Ab and Frank shouldered through. John halted them as he slowly stiffened, staring eastward down through the gloom of the yonder porch. A little red winking light lay out there, just beyond the porch's edge in the dust. He let off a bitter word, flung back the door and stepped out, dropped down and ran ahead.

Phil Chandler was lying face-down, half on, half off, Big B's porch, one hand flung ahead into the dust near where the faint-glowing cigarette lay. John dropped down, eased Chandler over and bent forward. It was difficult, in the layers of shadows on that porch, to make out old Phils' face.

Ab and Frank, then Jared and the others came up. None of them made a sound. Over behind the bunkhouse a man softly whistled. From inside the bunkhouse he got an answer. Samantha hovered close, but for a moment the men blocked her view. Then she got past them and sank down beside the sheriff. She looked swiftly into Wheaton's face.

'Is he . . . ?' she whispered, and John nodded.

'He's dead.'

Frank swung to go out where his saddle-booted carbine was slung on the off-side of his saddle. One of his men went out to also get a carbine. Two of Jared's rangemen came slipping up onto the porch from the west. The third Texan came along moments later, he was breathing hard, as though he'd been running, which he had, for this last Texan was the sentinel who'd had to come all the way up from down by the barn and corrals. When he saw Jared he said, 'Boss; they were on the skyline when one of 'em fired. I'd been watchin' but it was damned hard to be sure. I thought it was men hunkerin' up there, and had a bead on 'em. Then one of 'em saw this here feller come out of the house, build his smoke, an' when this here old man lit the match—he let him have it.' The Texan craned for a look downwards, and wagged his head gently back and forth. 'He never should've stood out there an' lit that match, boss.'

John eased old Phil back down and stood up to run a cold, careful look out along the skyline which lay northward and eastward. At his side Ab said softly, 'They're long gone, John. They think they got Jared, and they're long gone now.'

One of Jared's armed Texans growled in a low grumble he'd saddle up and go after them. John shook his head, bringing his dry stare around to that man. 'You wouldn't find them, but even if you did, and if they didn't hear you comin' and bushwhack you first, one man wouldn't stand a chance, cowboy; there are seven of them, counting Whitsett.'

Frank Arbuckle wasn't pacified by that and said, 'Then what do we do, John; just stand here?'

John didn't answer right away. He stood gazing down at dead Phil Chandler. A man comes into this world, he thought in the solemn coolness, works at trying to make his mark; at perhaps trying to turn out a

113

product—in Phil's case good saddles and sound harness—which will give comfort and satisfaction and long service to his fellowmen. Then he departs, and for perhaps fifty years afterwards his good works linger, then they too depart, and the sum and substance of the man's lifetime can be added up to just one thing: He helped time pass in the best and only way he knew to make it pass, so that for other men who came after him, the road was a little less rough, the labor slightly less arduous, and the moments of leisure slightly more pleasant.

Maybe that's what it was all about.

'No,' he said, coming back to a consideration of the present, and Frank Arbuckle's question, 'we don't just stand here. We'll take Phil over to the bunkhouse and lay him out, then we'll make out like we're headin' for town, just in case it wasn't too dark for them to spot our horses standin' over yonder at the hitchrack, an' we'll cut around and come straight on back—before daylight hits.' He stepped back and turned. 'Jared . . . ?'

Burcham nodded. 'Sure. Couple of you fellers pick up Mister Chandler and take him over to the bunkhouse, cover him up.'

'And turn out that light over there,' said John, turning back. 'Frank; Ab; you boys—let's go.' He led them out to their horses. Jared came along, hobbling on his sprained ankle. Jared said he'd take care of Phil's horse. He didn't ask John Wheaton what he had in mind or what his purpose was in wishing to return, until John, up athwart his saddle, leaned down and said,

'Jared; go on back inside. Leave a lamp lighted in the parlor. You an' Samantha keep out of sight an' away from the windows.' Jared nodded. Then John Wheaton said, 'You've just been killed, Jared. That's what they were waiting up there for, and that's what they think they accomplished. We want them to go right on thinkin' that. I'll see that the word gets spread around town. Damned if old Phil's just going to be sacrificed because Whitsett couldn't see whom he'd shot in the darkness. Phil's going to have the last laugh.'

He led them out of the ranchyard westerly, then swung southward and loped for a half hour before slowing and finally halting. 'Ab,' he said. 'Scout to the west. Frank; scout to the south. I don't think they even know we're out here, but I want to be sure of that.' He waited while his two friends rode off, then ran a speculative glance over the remaining men. He knew them; they were roustabouts and drivers for Arbuckle; tough, resourceful, dependable men. To the one whom he called Chet, he said, 'Listen close now, Chet; I've got a damned important job for you to do.'

The craggy-faced rider nodded. 'Spit it out, Sheriff; I'll do it.'

'Good. You go far south, then cut over to the east as far as the stageroad so they won't hear or see you, then ride on up into town. It'll be daybreak by the time you get there. Pass the word that Jared Burcham was killed last night on his porch out at Big B while he was smokin' a cigarette. Don't say you were out here. Just say you heard that from one of the Big B men. Keep passin' it around. You understand?'

Chet rubbed his grizzled jaw. 'I understand you want folks to figure Mister Burcham got it instead of old Phil, Sheriff, only I don't know *why*.'

'Because we want Carleton Whitsett to hear it, Chet. If he believes it, I'm betting he'll ride back to Big B, He knows Samantha will be the only surviving Burcham. We want him to think that; we want him to show up back at the ranch with his gun-crew.'

Chet's grizzled face brightened, finally. 'Sure,' he murmured, beginning to slyly smile. 'Sure as hell, Sheriff. An' you'll be lyin' in wait for him with the others. Right?'

'Plumb right, Chet. Can you hack your end of it?'

Chet nodded and raised his rein-hand. 'Depend on it, Sheriff. You just slip on back an' depend on me doin' my part.' Chet lifted his right hand in a little admiring salute, turned his horse and eased it around into the southward night.

The others sat in silence listening to Chet's departure, until Ab and Frank returned to report there wasn't a sign of Whitsett's gun-crew anywhere around, then they all turned their horses and headed back up towards Big B.

Chapter Thirteen

They came in from the west where darkness lay all around, eased quietly up into Big B's log barn, and put up their animals. They killed a little time forking feed and loosening girths, hanging bridles from saddlehorns and snugging up neck-ropes on their animals in the tie-stalls. After that, John led them around through the yonder gloom as far as the rear of the bunkhouse. It was there they came under four cocked guns. Jared's Texans had spotted them before they'd reached the yard and had hung back letting them have all the leeway they wanted, before closing in. When John identified himself, one of the Texans swore softly in bitter disappointment. He'd been hoping against hope, evidently, that it would be Whitsett leading in his gun-crew.

They approached the main-house from out back, because there was a distinct paleness beginning to brighten the eastern world, and if, as John said, Whitsett had just happened to be sly enough to leave a spy lying out there somewhere, he'd see them if they didn't keep the building between them and the yonder open country every foot of the way.

Samantha and Jared were waiting, in the darkened kitchen. She had her hair clubbed now, with that same little green ribbon John Wheaton had seen her wear once before. Jared had his carbine as well as his six-gun. He motioned them all inside, including his four rangeriders. In a low voice he said there was a fresh pot of java on the stove and plenty of cups at the table. But none of the men from town moved to avail themselves of this additional hospitality. They'd already had their fill, earlier.

John explained what he'd done about spreading the word of Jared's murder. The men—and Jared's handsome sister—stonily listened. They didn't interrupt as the sheriff also said he wanted every man to get under cover somewhere out across the yard.

'On both sides, if you can, boys, so's when they come in, we'll have them between two fires.'

'*When* they come in,' mumbled Frank darkly, 'or *if* they come in. John; I got m'doubts. Why would he try in the morning after he supposedly killed Jared? I tell you Whitsett's no fool.'

John agreed with that, but with one exception. 'Frank; every smart man is a fool in one thing. The trick is to find each man's blind spot. We've got enough evidence what's Whitsett's weakness; his hatred of the big cow outfits ruled by old families. Phil's over yonder in the bunkhouse, proof enough that Whitsett's a fool in this one respect. He'll come.'

Frank subsided, not necessarily convinced, but at least willing. Jared told one of his riders to take John's men outside and show them the places to hide. When Ab and Frank would've gone out too, though, Jared detained them, saying, 'It's still dark enough for some of us to get out on the range where we could stay out of sight behind a hill or down in an arroyo. What do you think, John?'

Wheaton was against that, particularly if Jared meant that he would ride out with the others. 'There are seven of them,' he explained. 'If you'n Ab, Frank and I went out to lie in wait, then hit them from behind, they'd see you, Jared, and turn on us.'

Samantha, silent up to now, nodded approval of what Wheaton had said, 'You're the only one they really want,' she told her brother. 'Why make it easy for them?'

Jared said no more on that topic. Ab and Frank left the dark kitchen for the slightly brighter night outside. Jared and his sister looked at Sheriff Wheaton. When the silence grew slightly awkward Samantha said, 'Sheriff; I know it's got nothing to do with any of this, but . . . we've seen each other so many times. . . . We've spoken. . . . But until last night I didn't know you.'

John gazed thoughtfully at the very handsome and also very strong-willed woman. What he thought was not at all what he said. 'I reckon that's understandable, ma'm. Our paths just never had much reason to cross, close up like this, before.'

She nodded, and kept studying. Outside, discernible through the windows, a very pale soft-tinted light began to filter over across the high heavens. There was a decided chill to the fresh new day, as there was every morning just ahead of dawn's first light. It was so quiet they heard some valley quail calling back and forth, their little pleasant sounds friendly, and lively with interest after the long night.

Out behind the corral a horse nickered, which brought all three of the people inside the house to a curtained front window where they commanded an excellent view of the shadowy yonder big ranchyard. But there was nothing to see; that horse evidently hadn't been greeting some strange beast, he'd been calling for his breakfast.

Samantha went into the parlor to blow out the lamp in there. As she returned she paused up close to John and softly said, 'There might be reason for our paths to cross now, mightn't there, Sheriff?'

He smiled a little, looking down into her strong face. 'There might be,' he assented, and stepped away to go across and join her brother who was leaning upon his carbine gazing through a window across the eastward range. 'See any movement out there?' he inquired. Jared shook his head. The land lay softly pink and endlessly hushed. There was no movement, no sound, no bright light even.

Samantha brought them both a fresh cup of coffee. She didn't smile at John this time; she appeared to be having trouble figuring him out. He was friendly without being warm towards her. He was pleasant and courteous. He seemed also to be distant. Her eyes narrowed in speculation.

'You're not married,' she told him. Her brother's eyes popped wide open. His coffee cup stopped mid-way to his lips. 'I haven't heard that you're even engaged, Sheriff. But maybe it's just that women frighten you.'

John's lips lifted thinly but he sipped his coffee while returning her narrowed look, without saying a word. Jared was watching his sister with an odd expression across his face.

Someone whistled. The sound carried only as far as the house. At once Jared put aside his cup, hobbled around and hoisted his carbine. 'The signal,' he said by way of swift explanation to John Wheaton. 'One of my men has spotted something.'

All three of them went to different kitchen windows, but none of them saw anything. John went out into the parlor and looked from there. He saw it, finally; a horseman walking his horse straight towards the yard from the blurry north.

'Samantha,' he softly called. 'Jared. Come in here.' When they came, John pointed far out. 'There he is.'

That soft whistle came again. It was answered from three different places around the yard. Jared eased all his weight down upon his good leg, and used his Winchester as a crutch while he made a long and very careful study of the oncoming horseman. Finally he said, 'I don't know him, John. He's no one from around here.'

Wheaton's retort was dry. 'You didn't expect him to be, did you? He'll be Whitsett's spy. He's comin' to see if Jared Burcham is truly dead. If he's convinced of it, Whitsett'll be the next one to ride into this yard—with his gun-crew.'

Jared twisted half around. 'And if we throw down on him and take him prisoner?' he asked.

John stepped closer to the window, studied the approaching man for a full sixty seconds, then stepped back again saying, 'Samantha; how good an actress are you? If that man sees you weeping and upset when you tell him your brother is dead, it might set the trap up for Whitsett to ride in.'

Before she could answer Jared said quickly, 'John; what about our riders? He'll smell a trap if there are none of the riders around, won't he?'

'No,' the sheriff replied, 'because Samantha sent them into town for the sheriff and the doctor. Remember; she only had half the crew here anyway.' He turned back towards Jared's sister, his eyes drawing out narrow in speculation. 'When was the last time you cried?' he asked. She replied that she'd wept when her father had died some years back, but not since then.

He'd been afraid of that. Samantha Burcham was made of iron, like her father had been and also like her brother was. She'd never be able to convince a sharp-eyed renegade she was actually in anguish. 'Go get an onion,' he said swiftly. 'Cut it in half and put part of it in your handkerchief. Hold it up to your face, Samantha. You'll cry. You'll cry so hard you'll be convincing.' She stood a second, staring, so John reached out, turned her and gave her a sharp little shove towards the kitchen door. Then she moved.

Jared sighed and threw an admiring glance upwards. 'Good thinking,' he murmured. 'Sam's just not the crying kind. She's too much like the rest of us.'

'Yeah,' muttered John Wheaton, looking after the handsome woman. 'That's the gospel truth, Jared. Too much like the rest of the Burchams.' Then, before Jared could ask what that meant, Wheaton turned back towards the window. 'He's in plenty good sight now, Jared. Take another look. He's one of that pair of amateur bounty hunters who rode in here yesterday morning looking for Lysle.'

Burcham leaned on his carbine straining far out where the cowboy was just entering the yonder yard, northward of the log barn. 'Be damned if you're not right at that, John,' he murmured. 'Maybe that answers the question about where Whitsett's getting his gun-crew.'

'There wasn't much "maybe" to it,' replied the lawman, and pulled Jared back from the window. 'If nothing happens now to upset things, we just might pull this off.' He turned as Samantha came back into the parlor. She'd loosened her hair; it hung in massive waves down past her shoulders. She was crying genuine tears too, into the little handkerchief she held to her face. John grinned at her. She didn't grin back; she couldn't. The fumes from the piece of onion in the cloth she held precluded that.

They pointed her towards the front door, then moved quietly over towards the other doorway, the one leading out of the big parlor into the pantry.

That oncoming cowboy made his way very slowly up towards the main-house. From a curtained little gloomy window in the pantry Jared and Sheriff Wheaton watched the man as he craned around from left to right as he passed up to the tie-rack out front, and sat his saddle for a moment as though the deep silence all around made him uneasy. They heard Samantha open the massive oaken front door and step out onto the porch. They couldn't see her; she never moved far enough forward from the door, but they had the cowboy's profile in their vision.

He removed his hat, sat a moment just looking, then he said something in a voice so low they couldn't hear his words in their pantry hiding place. They heard Samantha's choked-up reply though. She said Big B wasn't hiring right now; that someone had murdered her brother the night before and her foreman was in jail in Gatling; that hiring men right now was the farthest thing from her thoughts.

The cowboy pulled a long face and murmured what must have been something roughly sympathetic. He looked around the yard again, then asked another question. John could guess what it was he wanted to know this time, even before Samantha replied in a fading, quavering voice that she'd sent her riders into town to get the sheriff and the doctor. Then her shoulders shuddered, she stepped back unsteadily to lean upon the door casing, and cried into her handkerchief.

The cowboy considered her a moment, looked down into the dust, dropped the hat back onto the back of his head, said something else, and turned his horse to slowly ride back through the strengthening new light the way he'd come.

John let his breath out in a long sigh and wagged his head. He heard Samantha come back inside and close the parlor door. Jared was already heading back out there, but John lingered where he was for a while longer, keeping a watch on that retreating horseman. As the cowboy cleared the yard he hooked his horse over into a lope and grew steadily smaller the farther out he went, straight northward.

John finally went out into the parlor. Jared was sitting out there all alone. Samantha, he said, had gone to her room to bathe her eyes. 'That onion juice must be powerful stuff,' he chuckled. 'Now then, if we could just rub a little of it on their gunsights when they come next time, we'd have this battle half won.'

John sank down wishing for a smoke. The strain was beginning to tell on him. 'I need a drink,' he mumbled. Jared got up, limped out into the pantry again, and returned with a bottle and two shotglasses. He poured both glasses full, handed Sheriff Wheaton one, kept the other one for himself, and turned as someone came walking heavily in from the kitchen. It was Ab Folger, looking pleased and worried at the same time. Jared pushed his filled glass out towards the saloonman, but Ab shook his head. He wasn't in the mood for it.

'I was holdin' my breath,' Folger told John. 'Where's Miss Samantha? I got to compliment her. That act almost had me cryin' for her.'

John downed his straight-shot, blew out a big breath and leaned back in his chair. 'That's half the battle, Ab, if we convinced him. Otherwise—.'

'He was convinced,' Folger stoutly stated. 'Frank was hidin' with me out back o' the bunkhouse. Even Frank said it was the best piece of actin' he'd ever seen. Now then, John; how long before the others show up?'

Wheaton shrugged. 'If I could tell how Whitsett's mind works, Ab, I wouldn't be sittin' here. I'd be surrounding him, because I'd also know where he is.' John stood up morosely looking around. 'All I feel confident of right now is that it won't be too long before we see him this time, face to face. You'd better get back outside now, and be ready.'

Folger nodded, turned and departed from the room. Silence settled again, deeper and more oppressive than ever.

Chapter Fourteen

The sun arose. One of Jared's men went out to feed but the others kept their vigil. Sheriff Wheaton saw the bitter, hard flash of sunlight off a belt buckle or a carbine butt-plate, or perhaps a pistol, up in the loft opening of Big B's mighty log barn. He and Jared were standing by the large parlor window looking out when Samantha finally returned. Her eyes were still mildly inflamed but otherwise she'd recovered. When they complimented her she told them perhaps the next time they ought to weep with her. Then she went on through into the big kitchen and they could hear her rattling pots and pans.

Frank Arbuckle came through the house from the back to ask suspiciously if Jared and John Wheaton were sure they'd fooled that spy of Whitsett's. They were sure. Jared brought Frank a drink and the skeptical storekeeper mellowed a little. Actually, it was the waiting; it was getting to all of them. Even John's nerves were crawling.

Frank lingered only a little longer then retreated back through the rear of the house. They heard him in the kitchen speaking with Samantha before he eased back outside where the shadows still lay because the sun hadn't yet reached that rearward area.

Not long after Frank had left, one of Jared's tough Texans slipped in to report that he'd caught the white flash of reflected light eastward.

'Riders?' asked Jared, and the cowboy shook his head.

'Looked more to me like the reflection of sunlight off glass,' he said.

John Wheaton had the answer to that. 'Spyglasses. He's out there studyin' the ranch through spyglasses.'

'Then he's coming,' murmured Jared.

John ignored that and turned on the cowboy. 'You go down by the barn and tinker around out in plain sight. Fork some hay into the corrals and maybe haul a set of chain-harness out to fling across the tie-rack. Act normal. Act like you'd be doin' somethin' you'd do any day around here, but be sure you stay well in sight.'

The cowboy nodded and departed. After he was gone Jared said with a little indifferent shrug, 'What's the difference? With his binoculars, John, he can see every-thing's normal around here.'

Wheaton's answer was enlightening. It was also short. 'That's just the point. Everything *isn't* normal around here. You heard your rider; the spyglasses are over on your east range. That's towards town. Samantha told that spy she'd sent the crew into town for the law and the physician. If Whitsett's on the *east* range, that means he's darn likely already sent some men into town. They wouldn't see any Big B riders wanderin' around loose in Gatling. They'd report that to Whitsett. Now, unless he sees a man or two down here in the yard, he's going to know something's not right.'

As Jared digested this, Samantha came to the doorway and told them breakfast was ready. John asked if she'd made enough for the townsmen and rangemen outside hiding around the yard. She was ahead of him on that. She said she'd already sent food out, first with Frank Arbuckle, then with the cowboy who'd just left the house.

Jared had no more to say until the three of them were sitting down to eat. Then he told John he thought that unless a man was born to law work, it'd take a good many years for him to develop the ability to think two ways simultaneously; the way an outlaw thought, and the way a lawman had to also think.

Samantha refilled their coffee cups near the end of the meal. She offered to lace the java but both men declined. She went across to the stove, replaced the pot on its burner, and was turning back, her eyes set on the back of John Wheaton's head as though she had something to say, when a low, long whistle came to all three of them from the yonder yard. Someone out there had seen riders!

John arose, grabbed his carbine and hastened forward into the parlor. Jared hobbled along behind him and

Samantha came last. This time, though, those three could see nothing. Their view through the large parlor window was rather well limited to the northward. They could see slightly to their left and right, which was west and east, but the outbuildings cut off most of this sighting.

Jared said, 'From the east, probably. Sam; go look out the side-wall windows in the kitchen.'

Samantha departed at once. Again, that low whistle came, more insistent and careful this time. Whoever was approaching had to be getting closer. Someone out there in the yard let off a startled squawk. John and Jared exchanged a quick look. There was no mistaking the sound of surprise and alarm in that little unexpected outcry, but more than that, the man who'd made that outcry had endangered their entire plan by his noise. After that, though, the stillness settled again.

Samantha came back to breathlessly report that ten horsemen were coming towards the ranch from the east range. Jared said, 'Ten? Are you sure it's not seven, Sam?'

She was sure. 'Ten, Jared. They're riding in a wide line with several yards between each man.' She might have said more except that one of the Big B rangemen came rushing into the room to say there was a dust-cloud made by fast-moving riders approaching from far southward.

For ten seconds the four people in the parlor looked perplexedly at one another. 'Whitsett could've picked up another three men,' said Sheriff Wheaton finally.

'Instead of seven guns he could now have ten. It's possible; since yesterday more bounty hunters could have drifted into the country over those fake posters he had nailed up. If so, then the fact that he's comin' from the east may mean he recruited the new manhunters over in town.'

Jared's cowboy said, 'All right, Sheriff; but what about those other riders? You reckon he recruited more'n maybe just another three or four gunmen, an' split 'em up, one half to hit us from the east, the other half to come in from the—?'

'I sure hope not,' stated John anxiously, not permitting the Big B man to finish his statement. 'You sure those aren't just loose horses or maybe spooked cattle to the southward?'

The cowboy was sure. 'I didn't see 'em until Burl, who was hidin' with me out back o' the bunkhouse, looked aroun' an' let off a big squawk at sight of 'em. No sir, Sheriff; them's men—mounted men—an' they're comin' fast. Directly, the fellers approachin' from the east are goin' to see them too, if they don't already know they're comin'.'

There was, obviously, one way to discern whether Whitsett, riding to the attack from the east, knew the other band of horsemen, sweeping in from the south. He told the cowboy to go back outside and watch closely. As soon as the southward men were in close enough for everyone to see them, if they were more of Whitsett's men, he wouldn't falter, but if they were strangers to Whitsett, he'd stop out there to gauge

130

them, before making his next move.

It was a good plan, and it worked. The cowboy ran back outside where the heat was beginning to roll up over the land, and was gone hardly long enough for Jared and John, and Samantha, to fully discuss the possibilities which impended, then he returned a little breathlessly to report that the men coming from the east had seen the men rushing up from the south, and had halted out there in plain sight.

Jared was thoroughly mystified. 'Who?' he asked, looking from face to face.

No one answered. No one had a chance to. From far off came the unmistakable whiplash-sound of gunfire. John went to the front portal, opened it, stepped through with his carbine raised in both hands, and paced eastward on the pillared porch until he had a view of those ten fanned-out far riders. They were turning, were beginning to close up a little, rallying on a man farther out astride a chestnut horse whose coat glistened like new copper in the dazzling morning sunshine, shouting orders and gesturing southward.

John thought he had the answer to this expected turn of events and ran out into the yard yelling for everyone to get saddled up; to join him as he sprinted for the barn.

Men sprang up all around, lowered their Winchesters and dashed headlong in the direction John Wheaton had taken. Here and there a voice was raised in quick inquiry, but mostly, the men concentrated on reaching the barn.

For the townsmen, who hadn't off-saddled the night before, it was only a matter of a few moments to bridle, snug up their saddle cinches, and spring up over leather. For the Big B it took longer. They cried out for Sheriff Wheaton's men from town to wait. Jared was one of the last to reach the barn, hopping frantically on his good leg and brandishing his carbine as he yelled for someone down there to saddle him a horse.

John was fighting his excited horse down to a steady stand out in full sight beyond the barn as he watched those ten gunfighters out there on the eastward range spurring grimly away, southward. He thought it had to be some of those men who'd fired the shots heard earlier.

Finally, the Big B men began coming from the barn mounted and ready to ride. Samantha was over on the porch, hands to her throat, tensely watching. As John led the sweep of armed, excited men past, he yelled at her to get back inside and stay there. Maybe she heard him in the drumroll sound of shod hooves, and maybe she didn't, but in either case she didn't turn to re-enter the house for as long as any of them were in sight.

Frank Arbuckle and Ab Folger spurred up on each side of John Wheaton. Frank called over a question which was whipped rearward by the slipstream as they raced along. John thought he knew what Frank was asking about, but he didn't try to answer because of the noise they were making as they flung clear of the last building and broke over into a dead run heading southward straight for those strangers out there who were hauling down in their own dust, springing from their saddles and whipping their horses around to give them protection from the charge of Whitsett's hired guns.

A ripple of loose gunfire erupted from the embattled men southward. It stiffened up into a steady, growing staccato of lethal sound as Whitsett's riders bored straight in.

Other guns opened up, finally; Whitsett's riders returned that steady fire. John saw a man's horse violently jump, then fall, down among the southward riders. He saw another man turn his plunging animal loose, drop to one knee and return Whitsett's fire. But if the dismounted men had the advantage of being able to steady their weapons as they aimed and fired, they had the distinct disadvantage of shooting at wildly riding horsemen, the worst conceivable kind of targets to score against.

Whitsett's men weren't in any fairer way of overwhelming the strangers either, though, for the back of a plunging horse made the worst imaginable place to accurately shoot from.

But both sides stepped up their gunfire. The men on foot were woefully out-numbered but they stood fast, even refusing to take cover behind their horses, when the animals dropped around them.

Jared was yelling and spurring and brandishing his carbine. His bandaged ankle flopped, clear of the stirrup, and if he felt the pain at all he certainly gave no indication of it. He kept urging the men racing along with him to push on harder.

John was concentrating on gun-range. They were closing fast on Whitsett's men, up front and slightly to their left, but were still out of carbine range. Several of the Big B riders, though, suddenly began firing, tilting up their barrels hopefully, levering and firing. It was this sound which caused several of Whitsett's men to straighten in their saddles, twist half around in surprise, then let out cries of audible alarm. As those men slowed, John's crew rapidly bored ahead closing the intervening distance. He thought they were either within range or very close to it when he called out for the firing to begin.

At once gunfire crashed and roared all around, from out front, southward, where those doggedly fighting unhorsed men realized help was on the way, and to the east also, where some of Whitsett's gun-crew hadn't yet understood they were being attacked from behind as well as from in front, and finally, closing rapidly now and well within range, from the flaming guns of Sheriff Wheaton's crew, racing on up from the direction of the headquarters ranch.

Whitsett was out front. John saw him. So did Frank Arbuckle, who looped his reins, raised his carbine and concentrated hard on downing him. But Whitsett rode on, unhurt, and eventually, seeing that the tables had been turned; that he was no longer in command of this savage battle but was now out-gunned, Whitsett began yelling and waving his arms. When he finally swerved off easterly, his riders followed after, running their horses harder than ever to get out of range.

Several of John's riders swerved too, but he bawled out to them, signaling for them to come back. They did, but only very reluctantly. Frank Arbuckle lowered his carbine and fiercely swore as he watched the bounty-hunters under Carleton Whitsett draw off, putting more and more land between them and Frank's stubby-barreled saddle-gun.

Jared let off a high cry that resounded over all the other diminishing sounds of battle. John swung, thinking perhaps Burcham had been hit. But Jared was pointing rigidly ahead where those embattled men were standing up, were stepping from behind their horses, were looking around at one another, and over where three dead animals lay.

'Lysle!' Jared bawled at the top of his lungs. 'It's Lysle and my men from town!'

Jared was correct. When John slowed, and the others around him also hauled down their excited mounts, Lysle Small walked on out ahead of his other men, grounded his carbine and leaned upon it, watching the men from Big B lope on up. John and Ab Folger exchanged a look. Ab shook his head ruefully. 'Should've guessed,' he said across the little distance separating him from the sheriff. 'We sure as hell should've guessed.'

John agreed, but not out loud, as he reined down within a hundred feet of Lysle.

Chapter Fifteen

What had happened was understandable, once Lysle had explained it. The man named Chet whom John had sent back to town with the story of Jared Burcham's murder, had done his job well; so well, in fact, that Lysle's guardians at the jailhouse had heard the story and had rushed to Lysle with it. Big B's rangeboss's reaction was typical. He had his men release him, and had led them furiously towards Big B, determined to make certain Samantha was left under guard, after which Lysle said he'd proposed to take all but a couple of the Big B Texans, and go on a manhunt of his own—after Whitsett.

When he saw Jared, he indignantly demanded to know just what the hell was going on. After John and Jared explained, Lysle shook his head in strong disgust. He had, he claimed, not only spoiled John Wheaton's carefully laid plan to ambush Whitsett, he'd also scairt off the hired guns, and now, with three men on foot because their horses had been killed, he'd even precluded the possibility of a swift pursuit of Carleton Whitsett. He was angry, but all the anger wasn't directed entirely at himself. He was just as annoyed at not being told what the others had planned, even though, as John patiently explained, neither he nor Jared'd had time enough, nor the adequate opportunities, to ride back into Gatling and explain everything, because events had transpired too fluidly and too quickly.

One of the Texans riding with Lysle had been winged. Not seriously, but nevertheless painfully. A bullet had burned across the man's lower ribs, following on around with the contour of his body gouging the flesh. The injury was bloody but the man who had it, while stoutly denying he wasn't fit to go on, nevertheless weaved a little when he moved. The shock still gripped him.

There were six of them, counting Lysle, and only three horses left alive among those six. Frank Arbuckle, peering eastward from time to time during this interim, said it was only a short walk back to the ranch; a matter of perhaps a mile and a half or two miles. Even the wounded man could make it, he thought, but if not, then the other two could go on back, rig up a wagon and return for the injured cowboy. He then pointed where lazy dust hung high and listlessly in the bright, warm sunlight, saying he thought they should push on, not allow Whitsett to get away.

Ab was favorable. So were several of the other men including Lysle, whose horse had come through the battle unscathed. It was the murmurings of these men that sent Frank and Ab over to mount their horses. Frank's men from town looked dubiously from the sheriff to their employer, then decided to emulate their employer. They also went back, caught their horses and got astride.

John stood a moment gazing out where Carleton

Whitsett was swinging northward. He could no longer make out the riders, but thin tendrils of dust still arose. He turned to Lysle saying, 'Let's go.' Then he said, 'Jared; not you. Go on back and fetch horses or a wagon for your men. After that, stay with your sister.'

Burcham stiffly stared, indignation welling up strongly and obviously in him. When he replied he didn't use John's name as he always had up to now, he used his title. 'Sheriff; you don't give me orders in this matter.'

Frank and Ab turned to gaze downward. There had been that reedy sound to Burcham's tone men accustomed to violence quickly detected in the voices of other men. Lysle too, looked at the two men. John Wheaton was unperturbed. 'Like I said, Jared, you go back.' He stepped up over leather, twisted and glanced at the cowman. 'Those men aren't goin' to stop for a long while. Your ankle couldn't stand it. In case they *don't* stop, or they get sly and try cutting back, you'd better be home, Jared. I wouldn't put it past Carleton Whitsett to make war on women. I mean Samantha. I wouldn't put it past him to send someone back for a pot-shot either. Or maybe to burn you out.' John turned, switching his attention to the Big B rangeboss. 'Lysle; see to it he goes back.'

Jared was stiffly standing there when the others swung their mounts and started off, cutting diagonally across his range to eliminate some of the mileage Whitsett's men had taken in order to get far off easterly, before they swerved northward.

When they were a half mile out John turned to look back. No horseman was following them. He looked left and right, there were the townsmen, the five Texans who'd come from the ranch, and now there were two more. The last man was Lysle Small. He'd been detained a moment arguing with Jared Burcham. When he saw the way John was sizing up their little force, Lysle spurred on up to ride stirrup with him.

'Jared'll cool down, Sheriff. He's had a lot of pain an' excitement the past day or so,' said Lysle.

John nodded. He wasn't too concerned; his thoughts were fixed somewhere up ahead towards the sun-brightened foothills, and beyond them, towards the higher lifts and rises of the yonder broken and mountainous country. Whitsett had a destination in mind, there was no doubt of that, but whether his hideout was in the lower hills, or farther off, back in the dark and treacherous places of the uplands, was anybody's guess.

Frank acted differently now. So did Ab Folger. All that waiting and quiet back there during the long night had been hard on the nerves and senses. It was better for active men to be moving, to be riding, to be in pursuit instead of waiting to be attacked.

Cutting across the Big B range as they'd done brought John's crew into sight of fresher dust, up where the stageroad pass distantly twisted and turned its way down from the highlands, lying like a fresh gash between two clefts in the forested mountains. But they didn't see the riders, actually, although they loped steadily in an effort to see them.

Finally, the dust halted where the first tiers of trees began, and that, John said as he signaled for everyone to slow down and slacken off, meant Whitsett was going to stop soon, and look back, in which case he'd not only see that he was being persistently pursued, but he was also going to see that man for man and gun for gun, Sheriff Wheaton's party was stronger than his own party was.

Ab volunteered to take half the crew and slice off farther to the east. 'So's to cut 'em off if they keep tryin' to get out of the country,' Ab explained.

Frank Arbuckle was skeptical. 'From what I've seen of Whitsett lately, Ab, he's not goin' to run out just because some cowboys and townsmen slipped in behind him back there an' run him off. If anything, by my guess, that'll make him tougher and madder.'

John just plain didn't know; he hadn't yet been able to think ahead of Carleton Whitsett's actions very accurately, except once, which was his surmise that Whitsett would try to attack Big B, so right now, as he let his horse plod along, he tried to imagine what would be his best course. It was Lysle Small, slouching along with his eyes drawn out narrow as he studied that onward countryside, who gave them a clue as to what they'd do.

Lysle said, 'Sheriff; the way he's headin' will take him far enough back into the mountains we'd be a month smokin' him out—unless he only figures to get us up in there, lie over until nightfall, then slip back westward and come down behind us, which would put the whole country down below pretty much at his mercy, Big B included.'

John turned all this over in his mind and so did the others. When they came to a lift in the land, they halted while John asked some questions about that yonder high country. Lysle and the other Big B men, who'd ridden every inch of it, said there were hundreds of secret vales and glades up there, some even hidden beneath overhanging giant bluffs, where ten horsemen could hide without any inconvenience at all, while pursuers rode within a hundred yards and never even found their tracks.

Frank and Ab made smokes. So did some of the others. It was getting along towards mid-morning now. The heat was steadily increasing, some wheeling buzzards floated high overhead, dipping low now and then to study the band of horsemen, then began widening their sweep of the pale sky as they took in more and more land in their lazy spirals.

John dismounted and stood beside his horse. Ab and Frank also got down. Lysle, fresher than the others, said he'd make a little scout along the edge of their landswell and look out beyond it. No one objected so he left. One of the men who'd come from town with the rangeboss also rode off with Lysle.

Frank said, 'John; how long you been without sleep?'

Ab answered that succinctly. 'Too long. All of us have. What's wrong with lying down right here?'

There wasn't anything wrong with it, in John's view,

and he wouldn't have denied aloud that Ab was right; he *had* been too long without rest. His mind wasn't functioning right. Now, when he had a decision to make, he couldn't make it. Some of the other men dropped down in the pleasant warmth. They hadn't had much rest the night before either, but what they didn't know was that John Wheaton hadn't had any rest to speak of in three days and *two* nights.

He finally said, 'All right, Frank. We'll sleep a while. We'll still be out here between Whitsett and Big B, or the town either, for that matter, when he comes back down out of those mountains after sunset. If we went back to the ranch we'd just have to make this same ride anyway.' He lay back, tilted down his hatbrim to shield both eyes, and within two minutes was sound asleep. Frank looked at Ab with a little wry head-shake.

'Tough men got limits just like anybody else.'

Lysle came back to report there wasn't any movement up ahead in the yonder hills anywhere around. Ab explained what John had said and Lysle, gazing at the whisker-stubbled, sunken-eyed, rumpled peace officer, gently inclined his head. 'He's sure as hell earned it, boys, but while we're doin' this, suppose I head on back to the ranch for some grub?'

Neither Frank nor Ab objected particularly, although Frank thought that if anyone went back for food, it shouldn't be Lysle Small. 'Whitsett's boys aren't goin' to be the only ones abroad who'll see those blasted fake wanted posters, Lysle. Anyone can claim you as fair game from behind a tree or from belly-down in the grass. I figure you ought to send back one of your Texans, and the rest of us'll stay here behind this little rib of land an' graze our horses until sundown.'

Lysle didn't agree with that, especially, but neither did he argue very strongly against it, so in the end, one of the Big B riders was sent back, while the others went to care for their animals.

They were safe from immediate detection northward, as long as they remained behind their shielding hill. Since there was ample grass back there for the horses, they really had no reason to expose themselves. Whether Carleton Whitsett suspected they were somewhere down below him on Big B range, or not, didn't make a whole lot of difference. Unless of course he sent out a scout or two. Then their whereabouts would tell Whitsett what they planned on doing. For that reason two men, one in the grass to the west of their hill, one in the grass to the east of it, were kept on guard all the long, warm day.

Frank and Ab took turns napping. Ab got the most sleep because when Frank was awake he went among their men talking, explaining, showing a different side of his nature now and then by making the men laugh.

Thirst began bothering them shortly after the sun passed its meridian, but shortly before three o'clock the Big B cowboy they'd sent for food came back with four canteens and a bundle of food which Samantha had sent, along with a note for the sheriff from Jared. Frank debated about awakening the sheriff, and decided not to regardless of whatever might be in the note. It was just as well, because all the note said was that Jared apologized for getting a little edgy earlier in the day when John had told him to stay back at the ranch.

The men ate, drank, then either lolled back watching the horses, smoking or talking, or they drifted on out where the sentinels were lying, and joined in trying to catch some sight of movement up ahead where the foothills turned into mountain-slopes farther back, northward. In this manner the shank of the day passed, shadows began drifting in, thin and pale at first, then stronger and longer as the sun sank steadily lower, until finally Frank went over to awaken John. By then it was close to five o'clock, the sheriff'd had about six hours rest, and as he struggled up out of the limpness of total relaxation, he said, 'Any water around, Frank?' which showed he was no longer exhausted, but was instead thirsty and hungry.

He and Frank beckoned for Ab Folger and Lysle to come over. The four of them went over the surrounding lay of the land. John was familiar enough with most of it, but only in the general way a man would be whose duty had taken him across it many times without ever requiring him to become familiar with all its details and idiosyncrasies. But Lysle knew this Cheyenne Valley range by every yard and inch.

He said if Whitsett struck out for town they could see him come out of the yonder trees into the barren pass, providing Whitsett moved before full darkness fell. Lysle also told them that the only way he knew to prevent Whitsett from making another run on Big B would be to divide their force, station men over westward strung out to intercept Whitsett when he came out of the foothills after nightfall, and attack the manhunters before they, themselves, were detected.

This sounded good to all of them, although Ab was uneasy about dividing their force. All together they had enough men, probably, to rout Whitsett, even though Whitsett's men were seasoned gunfighters, and their companions were mostly ordinary-enough townsmen or cowboys. But if they split up, he said, Whitsett could ride right over the top of whichever band he bumped into.

John got up, beat dust off himself and said, 'The answer, Ab, is that neither party will get so far from the other they can't hear gunfire, if it comes. All right; let's catch the horses and split up.'

Chapter Sixteen

Frank Arbuckle and Lysle Small took half the men to ride west, over through the lengthening gloom across Big B's range to stretch a line of watchers between the hills and the lower, cow country.

Ab Folger and John Wheaton took the rest of the men over in the general direction of the stageroad. As they rode, they kept straining to see northward, where the sun no longer brightened that upland, shaded place, but where the very fact of the light, tawny colored earth showed fairly well even yet, hoping they'd perhaps be able to detect dark shapes and movement up higher through the mountains where the stageroad ran.

Ab eventually gave it up. So did one of the men riding with them who said, if Whitsett's gun-crew was coming down-country from that direction, the riders with Sheriff Wheaton were going to have to rely on their ears to detect them, and this is exactly what they did. John stopped every few hundred yards to listen, but none of them detected a solitary sound, except once when a coyote threw up its head and sang its quavering little song to the purple heavens.

They halted when full darkness descended, sat a while without a word passing among them, then went on once more, heading straight over towards the stageroad. They hadn't progressed a hundred yards when, without any warning, a rash of distant gunshots erupted in the westward night.

'That's it!' exclaimed Ab, wheeling his horse. 'John; they're comin' down out o' those damned westerly hills!'

John turned, as did the other men, and spurred rapidly in Ab Folger's wake. They had come perhaps two miles, perhaps slightly more than two miles, from where they'd originally parted from Frank, Lysle, and the riders accompanying those two men. Now, as they raced to close that gap, the sounds of gunfire stopped as suddenly as they had previously erupted. The only sound after that was the rush of hooves over the early-summer-hardened Big B range.

They'd covered the first mile, when the firing broke out again, but now it was coming from farther south, which made John think that Whitsett had broken through Lysle's and Frank's defensive line, and was undertaking a running fight as he led his men straight down towards Big B. He yelled at Ab and reined off on a southward-angling course. Ab and the others followed his example, understanding exactly what he had in mind—which was simply to save time by streaking it on this fresh tack so he could intercept Whitsett before any of them even got close to Big B.

It was a sound idea. Better than that, it was an admirable idea. John Wheaton desired to save Jared and Samantha Burcham from the wrath of that madman out there leading those hired gunmen. But it didn't work. Whitsett evidently stopped somewhere southward after breaking around Frank and Lysle, to listen, which was precisely what John had also been doing earlier simply because it was too dark to see. Whitsett had without doubt heard the fresh riders running in on him from the northeast. He now proved he was the match of Sheriff Wheaton or any other sagebrush strategist. He had to conserve his horseflesh and save his men if he could. Under the circumstances which he'd created by making his stubborn second run for Big B, there was just one way now to do that, and survive, because both he and his men could tell by the sound that the pursuit out there closing in from two sides, was overwhelming.

He gathered his men, bunched them with strict orders

to be quiet, to keep their horses quiet, until he gave the word, then, with John and Ab and Big B sweeping down upon him, Whitsett leveled his six-gun straight towards the oncoming sounds of horsemen, and fired. That was his signal. With a shout and a roll of pistol-shots, his gun-crew charged straight forward, not straight away, raking their horses from hip to shoulder as they hurled themselves straight at John Wheaton and his companions.

Ab saw them coming first but it was too late. He fired and cried out in alarm fighting to bring his plunging horse around. John and the others saw the muzzleblasts sweeping up, and simultaneously guessed that Whitsett wasn't running at all—at least he certainly wasn't running away from *them*—but they and the astonished men around them had the same trouble Ab'd had. They couldn't fight their horses around soon enough. Whitsett was on them before they could even break off and run for it, every man for himself.

But Whitsett made a mistake too. When he and his yelling gunmen hit, they fired left and right, twisting one way and another in their saddles, but they did not stop. Whitsett led them furiously right on through and on past, out into the shadowy night.

Abner Folger tried twice to pick off Whitsett, and the second time was concentrating so hard he didn't see the man rushing him from behind. John Wheaton saw the blinding flash without fully understanding. His men were screaming in the same excited way Whitsett's gunmen were also yelling. Between this wild confusion, the deafening crash of guns, both pistols and carbines, plus the uncertain light of the night, no one could be certain of anything except that twisting, writhing shapes were mixed briefly in a life-and-death struggle, then what seemed a lifetime was suddenly ended as Carleton Whitsett led his men away again.

They didn't get very far before Lysle Small and Frank Arbuckle, mauled from an earlier meeting with Whitsett's gunmen, swerved in from the north and rolled a red-flaming volley of thunderous gunfire out across the dark and intervening distance. John heard a man cry out, his voice high and keening in the aftermath of that lethal volley, then it was choked off and the only thing to afterward be heard, was the echo of that savage volley.

It was over. As in all such wild, confused and confusing fights, no one was ever afterwards sure just how long it had taken. Everything each of those men would stake his life upon—*had* staked his life upon, good or evil, right or wrong—had been telescoped into that one deafening, blinding crush of men and horses and gunfire.

Lysle's crew ran on up, carried forward by their momentum. Frank Arbuckle cried out his name several times to eliminate, if possible, someone's wild, sound-shot. John called to the men scattered back around him to hold their fire. Somewhere eastward came the diminishing roll of hooves where Whitsett's gun-crew continued on through the easterly night.

John called towards several visible riders, fighting

their panicky mounts down to a steady control, asking Lysle and Frank if they'd been hurt. Neither had, but when they came on up and halted, Frank pointed around. There were two riderless horses trailing along with them. 'Up north,' Frank said flatly. 'Those two got it when Whitsett first came onto us. John; he never stopped. Never even slowed down. He hit us like a regiment of cavalry an' kept right on goin'.' Frank stopped, made a little dry cough deep in his throat, then quietly and steadily swore.

Lysle dismounted stiffly looking around. John did the same, which set the example; they all dismounted. From farther back one of the Big B called softly for John to walk on back.

There were four men leaning and one down on his knees beside baby-faced, burly Abner Folger. Ab wasn't moving; John bent in the poor light to look closer, but Ab's eyes were closed and his chest seemed quite still. The Big B cowboy who was kneeling quietly said, 'In the back, Sheriff. I'd say from not more than fifty or a hundred feet.' The cowboy raised Ab's torn shirt to show the torn flesh high up and its gelatin, raw look, then gently lowered the shirt again.

Frank Arbuckle sank down and put his ear to Ab's chest. In a hushed and astonished tone he shot a quick look upwards at John saying, 'He's alive. He's still alive, John!'

They gathered in close, all but two men Lysle sent to look after their horses, and combined their skill at this kind of thing to staunch the flow of blood and make a bandage. Then they bathed Ab's gray face and made him as comfortable as they could.

John asked Lysle to send a man to the ranch for a wagon. 'Have him put plenty of straw in the bed, and fetch back some blankets as well. We'll take Ab on back to town.'

Lysle was grim and dogged when he turned to pass these orders to one of the Big B rangeriders, then he asked John to walk back with him a short distance, and out there with just the two of them, he pointed to a pair of dead Texans.

'Hell of a high price to pay,' he said stonily. 'Those were good men. I've lived in the same bunkhouse and eaten at the same table with them for a long time.' Lysle stood like a statue gazing at the sprawled corpses, leaning upon his carbine. John stood with him saying nothing for the elemental reason that there was just nothing a man could say. Someone sang out from the eastern range a little distance off.

'Hey; if anyone's interested, we got one. He's lyin' out here.'

John left Lysle to go along with several other men who were converging on that place where the dead gunman lay. The minute he saw that still face, he winced. That was the down-at-the-heel young cowboy who'd originally ridden into Big B's yard asking about a man named Lysle Small, with his pardner. The same one who'd returned much later, after Phil Chandler's murder, to spy for Carleton Whitsett and listen to weeping Samantha Burcham's tearful story of her

151

brother's pseudo-killing.

Frank was there. He said, 'Know him, John?'

Wheaton nodded. 'I've seen him a couple of times before. Young buck down on his luck lookin' for any way to pick up a dollar.'

Frank wasn't sympathetic. 'Well; he didn't quite make it. All he picked up was about a half cent's worth of lead.' Frank turned and went pacing back through the night over where the majority of the surviving men stood, or knelt, around unconscious and gravely injured Ab Folger.

The miraculous thing, although right at the time no one heeded it, was that although there had been horses everywhere during the fight, before it and even after it, not one horse had been killed or even creased with a bullet. Later, the men who lived through this bad night would sit around in town at the *Antlers Saloon* and recall such a bizarre thing, but right then they drained the last of their canteens, made cigarettes with unsteady hands, and when Lysle came over, mounted his horse and reined up to John Wheaton, they look and listened.

'Goin' to track 'em by sound if I can,' he said bleakly. 'Don't tell me not to, John. This time they don't get away. I'll signal with fire, if I can, after daylight comes, or else I'll heliograph with my belt-buckle. But I'm goin' to camp on their tails.'

John nodded. He had neither the wish nor the authority to prohibit Lysle Small from what he meant to do. If he thought even for a moment one of the other men, for whom Carleton Whitsett had no special hatred, might be safer at this manhunting, he didn't mention it. All he said was, 'Good luck, Lysle. We'll take care of Ab and your two dead riders, then get fresh horses and hit the northward trail, watching for your signals.'

Lysle raised his reins and looked long at John Wheaton. 'Maybe it'd be better if you stayed at the ranch, John, an' just sent me my Big B riders.'

John understood perfectly what was behind that remark. Big B would systematically and ruthlessly destroy Carleton Whitsett and every man they caught in his company, according to the law of the range, not the law of the courts. 'I'll come too,' he said, his face wiped clean of any indication of which way he might right then be leaning. 'Like I said, Lysle—take care.'

He stood a moment listening to the soft hoof-falls as Lysle rode off into the cooling night, then Frank came over smoking a cigarette, solemn and tired and wrung-out, to also gaze outwards. Without taking his eyes off the fading onward silhouette of Lysle Small, down the trough of the northeastward night, Frank said, 'John; we won't need the blankets an' the straw in that wagon from Big B. Ab's dead.'

The men back there were like carved stone, all but one, who was stiffly arising as John came on up. He shook his head. 'It shouldn't have happened,' this townsman said roughly and softly, 'but it did happen. How do you account for a decent feller cashin' in like this, Sheriff?'

'I don't,' spoke John, gazing at the relaxed,

smoothed-out face of his dead friend. 'But I reckon if one man will stay here and wait for the wagon, there's no need for the rest of us to wait around, now. Ab and those two Big B riders don't need us now. Not standin' around here.'

The men nodded and muttered and turned to shuffle off towards their horses. They were tired and hungry and thirsty, but now and then in the hard environment of men such as these, hatred and deep resolve could eliminate all other sensations.

Frank dropped his smoke, ground it out underfoot, cast a final, dark gaze upon Ab Folger, then turned to also go out where the horses were.

John stopped him. 'There wasn't any real reason for this,' he murmured. 'Big B didn't want a fight; Ab an' you an' old Phil, an' I—we didn't want a fight. But it came anyway.'

Frank gazed a moment at the younger man before he quietly said, 'John; one way or another, with guns or pieces of paper or transits, or even books, men fight. Don't ever believe what those poet-fellers say; there's nothing basic in this damned world but competition—whether with words or guns. To survive is to fight every damned lousy day you're here on this globe. Now come on; there's *one* fight I want to get at, before I go back to town and get drunk—an' *stay* drunk for a damned lousy week.'

They left one townsman with the bodies, rode off in a clutch of bunched-up, haggard, coldly resolved armed men honed to a killing edge by adversity and by the senseless death of some very good men. Their time of tactics and planning was all past. They wanted to find and destroy an enemy, and that's *all* they wanted.

There was no sign of Lysle Small up ahead. He'd evidently ridden faster and farther than John thought. Nevertheless, they kept heading northeastward towards the high country, confident that's where they'd find their enemies one more time.

Chapter Seventeen

Dawn came, as it always did, bringing light and, after a time, warmth as well. They found Lysle Small's tracks by the simplest of expedients: They scouted for Whitsett's tracks first, found them, then picked out the separate fresh sign of another ridden horse passing along parallel to Whitsett's sign. It was that simple.

They were deep into the foothills before daylight. After daylight they were into the first fringe of forest, which ranged easterly and westerly all up and down the Cheyenne Mountains. They rode silently and doggedly, no longer out-numbering Whitsett's gun-crew, but no longer much concerned about this either.

John was directed by one of the Big B men to a spring where they all watered their stock, filled up themselves, then rested briefly while Frank Arbuckle and one of his teamsters scouted on up-country a little distance on foot. While they rested Sheriff Wheaton shared his tobacco with a Texan, and was told that unless they kept on the tracks they'd never find their prey up in this fragrant, shadowy country of pines and firs and spruces. The Texan made a sweep with one arm, eastward and northward.

'As far yonder as the stageroad it's fairly easy country to find things in—men or horses or cattle. But due north it gets rough—in some places even too rough for horses—and it's shot through with them potholes folks say was caused a million or so years back, by explodin' bubbles of cooling lava.'

John said, 'Water . . . ?'

The Texan smiled approval. 'Sure-'nough, Sheriff; men can't stay away from waterholes too long. 'Specially if they got sweatin' horses under 'em. But up here it isn't just a matter of stakin' out ten men at ten springs. There are more cussed little piddlin' creeks comin' down off the ridges an' out o' the blessed rocks, than a man can count.' The Texan squinted up where Frank and his teamster had disappeared, then went on speaking. 'Now, down in Texas, or over in the Arizona country, like you was figurin' a moment ago, all folks got to do is get settled beside a waterhole an' directly everyone'll come past. But this isn't Texas or Arizona.'

John was letting his horse pick grass; was holding the animal by its reins and gazing off up through the trees having trouble shaking off a pall of private gloom. He didn't see Frank and the teamster until the lanky man standing there with him grunted and jerked his thumb out where a pair of speckled wraiths passed in and out of tree-shade. Then John saw them. He could tell even from that distance, that Frank had seen something. He handed the Texan his reins and went forward.

Frank stopped, waiting, and said something to his companion. The teamster nodded and walked on down where the other men were resting. As soon as John came up, Arbuckle rolled his head on his shoulders to indicate the trail he'd just come down, saying, 'Smoke back up there. We saw it from a clearing. Just a pencil-thin stand of it risin' straight up.'

'Coffee fire?' asked John, and Frank shook his head.

'Too small even for that,' he said. 'I'd guess it to be Lysle Small. It's risin' above the trees up there about where a feller like the rangeboss would make his fire, knowing it'd be visible for a long way southward on a still, clear day like this.' Frank started down towards his horse. 'Let's get moving. I'll lead the way.'

John nodded and turned. They walked perhaps a hundred feet, then Frank stopped, throwing the onward men a careless gesture to mount up. He turned one more time, facing John Wheaton. This time his hawkish, shrewd eyes were speculative. 'John,' he said quietly, not permitting his words to travel very far. 'I heard what Lysle said last night, about maybe you'd be better off back at Big B, or back in town.' Arbuckle paused picking his next words with care. Down through the trees the others were getting astride, pulling their horses around. 'I want you to understand something about me,' he went on saying, in the same soft way. 'I'm as much for law an' order as the next man. I happen to be a mite older'n the rest of you fellers; happen to have seen all kinds of law in my time.'

John broke in with mild impatience. 'If you're workin' up to ask me whether I favor lynching Whitsett when we find him, the answer is—no.'

Frank looked a moment at the ground, said not another word, and stalked on down where his horse was being held by one of the townsmen. He got astride and led out. When he passed John he looked down once, gave his head a sad little disapproving shake, then moved on past.

They went on up the fresh trail as before, only now the land heaved and tilted more, showed more stark rock outcroppings, more underbrush and now and then, a little greeny glade with buck tracks and cat-prints where the shady earth was soft. Finally, they detected the scent of wood smoke.

Frank skirted a little meadow, cut completely around it moving eastward, and halted finally where a craggy ridge of naked dark stone divided the land from north to south. Ahead of them on a height of this rocky rib, they saw Lysle Small's fire, but after that, as they doused the last embers from one of their refilled canteens and struck out over Lysle's tracks, they saw at once that Whitsett's tracks, just as fresh and numerous as before, turned abruptly and ran down a steep slope into a fold in the lower hills.

John halted. Frank eased up beside him in the dark place, and rubbed his jaw. 'Which way,' he asked, 'after Whitsett or after Lysle?' When John turned from studying the sign and looked far off down into the lower, upended country, without at once replying, Frank said, 'Lysle's up to something. He'll do better on his own.'

John agreed, but for a different reason. As long as Whitsett's tracks had been before them, there'd been no chance of losing out, even through the mattress of pine needles, but the chances that they'd lose Lysle's solitary tracks up in here were very good, in which case they'd also lose precious time because then they'd have to back-track to Whitsett's sign, and go on from there.

John turned back. 'Whitsett's sign,' he said, and led the way back to that steep slope where the tracks led downward.

One of the Texans said, 'Sheriff; if they're down yonder an' just happen to look up this cussed slope, they're goin' to spy us sure as the day is long.'

John was also aware of this. 'Any other way to get down into that grassy watershed beside this slope?' he asked, and when the Texan only shrugged, meaning if there was such a way he didn't know of it, John kept right on riding.

There were trees on the slope, but they were spaced at long intervals, so the possemen were exposed about half the way down, or, looking at it from another viewpoint, *some* of them were *always* exposed because they had to ride in single-file down the game trail, precisely as the men they were chasing also had to descend this same trail.

If anyone down there happened to be watching,

they'd be spotted without doubt. John understood when he was part way down why Lysle hadn't taken this same trail. Alone, with nine deadly foemen somewhere down there through the trees probably drawing beads on him, he'd never have reached the bottom. So Lysle had chosen to scout around through the easterly hills and trees for another approach to the watershed canyon.

But they were half way down and nothing had happened before John twisted in the saddle to glance backwards and upwards. Frank Arbuckle was at the tail end of their line, riding heads-up. The townsmen, less accustomed to these steep, precipitous trails than the Texans, weren't nearly as anxious about danger from below, judging from their pale faces, as they were of one misstep by their mounts.

Frank signaled ahead to John Wheaton that all was well. John squared up again, riding on a loose rein and leaving the navigation of their dusty trail to his mount, which was the best course to follow, and in this manner came within sight of the last hundred yards, and yonder, where the trail abruptly ran out into a tall stand of emerald grass. That was where the watershed canyon began. In ages gone, some gigantic wall of water had once come down through there slicing away rock and hurling boulders hundreds of feet, like pebbles. The result was a pleasant, grassy place, with horse-sized rocks scattered up along the meadowlands against each side of the slopes. The creek now running through this place, from west to east and disappearing around a far bend into the yonder forest again, was swift and white-capped; evidently the fall was greater than it looked. Actually, the meadow seemed nearly flat from up the trail, but as John Wheaton got closer to the end of their dusty pathway, the land loomed up in proper perspective. It wasn't flat at all, but was formed into rolling low swales, not seemingly higher than perhaps fifteen feet, and all formed crossways to the canyon, or from north to south.

The gunshot which came, finally, sounded both distant and somehow tardy. It should've sounded flat and deadly; instead, its echo drifted upwards in fluting waves, softened no doubt by imprisoning canyon walls, and diluted by the distance from which the gunman had fired.

John kicked out his horse and stumbled, slid, and scattered pebbles the last few yards. He whipped backwards to see if the others had been hit. Evidently no one had, but they were all pushing their mounts now, even the height-conscious townsmen, for clearly that gunman was across the creek somewhere north of them in among the gloomy forest, where he could lie prone, take his rest upon a rock or perhaps an old deadfall log, and shoot at them as though they were grouse sitting on a tree limb.

Frank Arbuckle's profane growl at the man dead ahead of him was the only sound for a moment or two, then another gunshot sounded, and two more, as though that hidden sentry over across the creek in the trees had brought up reinforcements.

John didn't look back again after he reached the meadow until he'd spurred swiftly over alongside one of those rolls of grassy land. There, both he and his horse were safe. He turned after dismounting, carbine in hand, to watch the others. They covered the last few yards in a swift rush, struck the valley floor and whirled out over towards him, wrenching out carbines as they came. Frank Arbuckle was the last man down. Another of those lazy-sounding gunshots came. That time, John saw the puff of dust where a bullet struck. Frank saw it too, and dropped down alongside the neck of his mount. That bullet hadn't missed him by more than ten inches, which was very good shooting under the circumstances. So good, John thought, whirling to locate the drift of gunsmoke where those gunmen were, that unless someone diverted that marksman over there, the next shot just might knock Frank out of his saddle.

Two of Lysle Small's Big B men flung off, hit the ground sprinting ahead, and hurled themselves down in the grass, facing across the creek. John picked up the drift of gray smoke across the creek, raced part way up their shielding low hill, dropped to one knee and levered off three rounds as fast as he could work the Winchester's mechanism, and squeeze the trigger.

He accomplished his objective. The hidden gunmen over there held off firing just long enough to permit Frank to reach the protective shelter where the others were, and drop out of his saddle cursing and brandishing his carbine. Frank was mad clear through.

John got down flat, as the others were also doing, and waited for a fresh puff of dirty smoke to tell him where a rifleman was, across the creek. He didn't see one. No more gunfire came, the silence settled once more, and Frank panted up to throw himself down beside the sheriff and blisteringly denounce anyone, particularly Carleton Whitsett, who had to fight from cover 'like a damned redskin!'

John plugged fresh loads into his Winchester and looked back. Two Big B men were catching the horses to prevent them from wandering out where they could be seen, and shot at, from across the creek. He also made a slow survey of where his riders were. Thanks to the tall grass in this hidden canyon, the men were very nearly invisible, down in it.

Without any hint in advance, a furious burst of gun-fire erupted across the creek. Frank dropped his head and swore with great feeling. The others also flattened out in the grass. John waited, then raised up; something was bothering him. For all that gunfire and activity over yonder, no bullets were striking close by, which was definitely a mystery since Whitsett's gun-crew had already proven itself very competent with weapons.

Chapter Eighteen

'Hell,' growled Frank, following John's example by raising up just enough to look out over the tall grass. 'They aren't shootin' over here at all.'

163

John dropped down. 'Lysle,' he muttered. 'They're firing back up through the trees behind them. Lysle must have sneaked around them and opened up during the exchange, from farther back.'

Frank snapped his jaws closed and peered out again. The gunfire from across the creek was turning sporadic now, turning deliberately high and searching as Whitsett's men fired up the hill behind them. 'Random shootin',' Frank said, and a hundred feet away one of the Texans said practically the same thing.

'They don't know where he is, so they're sluicin' bullets all aroun' up through them cussed trees yonder.'

That yonder gunfire was so vicious and sustained, John began to worry that despite his excellent protective cover northward, Lysle might be hit anyway, so he called around him to the watching, speculating, men.

'Let 'em have it. Hold your fire low. Don't shoot high or we may hit Lysle before they do. Let 'em have it!'

These men with John had been a long time in preparation for this particular moment. When they'd met Whitsett's crew before they hadn't really had a chance to prove anything except that they *would* fight. Now, they had an opportunity to show that they *could* fight. Frank let fly with the first round. John joined him, then all the other men around them in the grass, and over closer to the flank of their low hill, opened up. For some little time the noise was deafening. Evidently it was also disconcerting, because the gun-crew across the creek turned back to this more formidable, southward enemy, and left off shooting into the rearward

164

forest where Lysle Small was sniping.

When the tumult gave signs of slackening off, John would call out for his companions to keep it up, to burn their bullets into the yonder low underbrush where those bounty hunters and their venomous employer were hiding. For a full five minutes the battle raged back and forth until the manhunters across the creek began to slacken their fire even though John's men never did slacken off.

Now and then, with soiled gray smoke drifting above their hideouts over through the forest beyond the creek, someone would cry out at the top of his voice. The men with Sheriff Wheaton heard these yells and wondered about them. One thing they were *not,* were shouted orders from Carleton Whitsett for his men to keep firing. Or, if they were, his men weren't paying much attention to them, for the gunfire continued to dwindle from across the creek.

John beckoned Frank Arbuckle over to him, sent Frank back with words for their companions to keep up the fierce firing while Sheriff Wheaton and Frank Arbuckle crawled through the grass to the bank of the creek where they might be able to actually see, and pick off, a gunman or two, and to be damned certain to keep their sights above the yonder creekbank.

Frank didn't demur either time. When he came back and started belly-crawling ahead through the grass he actually turned once and grinned at Sheriff Wheaton. He was a crusty old-timer who feared neither man nor the devil.

John had picked their route while he'd been lying near the top of that rearward low hill where the others were still throwing lead, raking back and forth, up and down, the underbrush-shelter and yonder big trees where their enemies were pinned down. He'd first decided to try this crawling forward when he'd spied a low swale at the creekbank, deep enough, providing they didn't raise up, to comfortably protect two fair-sized men. He kept angling along towards that ancient bear-wallow, or whatever it was, and finally rolled down into it. Frank eased over the edge and also slid down in.

For ten seconds they simply lay there breathing hard. The crawling hadn't been particularly strenuous, but the excitement and tension certainly had been.

From across the creek that dwindling gunfire began to brisk up again, as though Whitsett and his men were piqued by the galling fire Big B's rangeriders, and John Wheaton's townsmen, were pouring at them. It was this stiffening of the fighting resolve of the gunfighters that kept John and Frank pressing flat down in their bear-wallow, because every now and then a bullet would come slashing through the grass nearby.

For some little time this savage and stubborn little battle persisted, then Whitsett's men began crying out to one another. John heard that and looked at Frank, who looked back making a little grimace. Frank pushed his head close and yelled over the thunder of guns that Lysle Small must've picked one of them off from back up there in the forest.

Frank was probably correct, because once again the manhunters divided their gunfire between the southward and northward areas. Every now and then one of them would cry out in unmistakable alarm. John parted the grass very gently to look across the creek. He saw men jumping frantically from one sheltered place to another. He turned and nodded at Frank. That was it, all right; Lysle was spotting them from behind.

John eased his carbine out, took a solid rest with his elbow solidly planted in the earth, waited until one of those hiding gunmen had to jump away, and fired. The bounty hunter let off a high cry which ended abruptly as he dropped his carbine and pitched forward to fall across a punky old deadfall pine, and lie limply there.

Frank poked his Winchester out, too, and fired twice into the foremost brush patches across the creek. His first shot flushed a bounty hunter, sent the man tumbling backwards in a wild scramble to get behind a tree, but his second shot missed entirely.

The Big B riders and their companions from town began edging up through the grass also, bound for the creekbank. They fired sporadically as they advanced. It was this firing, low and persistent, which drove Whitsett and his hired guns deeper into the forest. But that was a definite mistake too, for at once they began to wince away from bullets coming down from behind them. Lysle Small seemed well supplied with ammunition, and also well supplied with the cold and vindictive wrath which kept him unflinchingly up where he was as those withdrawing gunfighters came back towards him.

They turned and desperately tried to find Lysle, to kill him or at least to dislodge him from their rear-line. Lysle would move left and right, sometimes backwards, then forwards again. He was like a wraith; they'd fire at his muzzleblast only to get back another shot from him in a totally different position. He seemed to possess a charmed life.

John waited until the others were close to the bank of the creek, too, then yelled for them to fire and keep firing. He set the example. Frank did the same. They'd had ample time to freshly fill each slide of their carbines. Now, once more, the tumult rose to a thunderous crescendo. Bullets sped both ways, but because of the demoralization setting in over across the creek, accuracy from that side suffered. For sixty seconds this fierce and unrelenting fight continued, but neither flesh nor bone could withstand this kind of a battle indefinitely, so John wasn't too surprised when one of the men over there with Carleton Whitsett began crying out that he quit, that he'd had enough.

It was this man's loud and profane yelling which seemed to hasten the total demoralization of his companions over yonder. Their firing dwindled down to an occasional gunshot. John leaned and brushed Frank's shoulder, shaking his head. Frank glared for a moment longer, tugged off one more shot, then removed the carbine from his shoulder while all around them in the grass the others did the same. After another long sixty seconds, all the firing ceased.

In some ways the silence which ensued was louder, more threatening, than the gunfire had been. No one moved; no one dared to move, for whether they were shooting or not, every man knew other men were waiting and watching for such movement.

John called out. 'This is Sheriff Wheaton from Gatling. You men over there with Whitsett put down your guns and walk out of those trees!'

No one obeyed. John hadn't really expected them too. Not with Lysle still hiding back there with his ready guns. Frank grunted, wiped sweat off his flushed face and shook his head at Sheriff Wheaton. 'They're not whipped yet,' he muttered.

John thought otherwise. 'Lysle,' he sang out, louder. 'Hold off. Give them a chance to quit.'

There was no answer to that, but John hadn't expected any. Finally, though, that same high-sounding and profane voice they'd all heard before yelling out for quarter, yelled over to John from somewhere up in the yonder gloom. 'Hey Sheriff; get him out'n behind us an' some of us'll walk out. But you got to do that first; he's murderin' us—whoever he is.'

John didn't call back to Lysle for a moment. He instead looked left and right to see where his own men were. They'd been using this truce-time to inch always closer to the edge of the creek. If the fighting began again, they'd be in perfect position to sluice the area where the gunmen were.

John finally said, 'Hey, Lysle . . .'

A gunshot sounded from back through the trees. Just

one shot. It sounded louder than all the other gunshots combined had sounded earlier because of the deathless silence all around. Frank said, 'That was *him*. John; he's murderin' 'em.'

One of the Big B men called over in a voice made almost pleasant with cold satisfaction: 'Yonder goes another one. That'll help settle for our two.' The Texan was apparently referring to the pair of Big B men killed earlier, when the gun-crew had ridden over the top of Lysle and Ab Folger, killing two men as they did so.

'Lysle!' sang out John Wheaton. 'That's all! You shoot that gun once more an' you'll be in as much hot water as *they* are in!'

This time the answer came floating softly down from back up in the dark forest. 'No need, John. It's all over.' Then Lysle said, 'You scum down there with Whitsett; stand up and step out where they can see you—without any damned weapons!'

Lysle's icy command brought more response than all John Wheaton's words had, despite the fact that John had plenty of guns to back up what he said. One of the gunfighters over there beyond the creek cried out that he was obeying, and gingerly stepped from behind a bullet-marked big fir tree, both hands high above his head.

John raised up to cover that man. 'All the rest of you now,' he ordered. Very gradually, depending upon their degrees of caution, the other bounty hunters eased forward, all with their arms high, all of them fearfully rolling their eyes from front to back.

John said, 'Frank; you and I'll wade over.' He raised his voice so everyone, even Lysle Small, could hear him. 'Two of us are coming over. The rest of you keep your guns up and cocked. If one of them makes a wrong move—kill him!'

Arbuckle arose stiffly and truculently, leaving his Winchester in the grass, palming his six-gun exactly as John Wheaton also did. They stepped down into the creek, and winced; that water was straight off a snowcap somewhere. It was cold enough to numb their feet and lower legs before they got across and stamped up onto the far bank.

There were four men standing out in plain sight as they advanced, six-guns held low and cocked. Farther back through trees and shadows, came Lysle Small, stalking forward, also with his six-gun in hand. But Lysle didn't pay much attention to John and Frank, nor to the four disarmed, surrendering bounty hunters. He was watching one particular place, where two sturdy chaparral bushes seemed to be growing out of the same root-stock. He cut across directly towards that spot.

John saw how Lysle was crossing over and shot a look in that direction too, but there was too much brush for him to be able to discern anything. Then his attention was caught as Frank growled. ' 'Got to be more'n just these four, John. There was nine got away from us in the dark last night.'

But the closer they got to those four, the more it became apparent where the others were. One was draped over a deadfall tree-trunk where one of Sheriff

171

Wheaton's bullets had dropped him. From around a close-by tree was an outstretched hand and arm, palm up, six-gun lying nearby. Sprawled between two pines was another man. He'd been caught in mid-jump and riddled.

Back across the creek the townsmen and Big B riders were cautiously getting up out of the grass, holding their carbines at the ready. No one spoke a word. John and Frank walked back and forth counting the living and the dead. All nine men were accounted for, and oddly enough, there were no wounded. Whitsett's bounty hunters were either uninjured and alive, or they were stone-dead.

Lysle Small arose from behind that chaparral clump and quietly called to John. He and Frank went over there. Lysle pointed to the man propped against the bushes and said dispassionately, 'That last shot I fired—I'd been tryin' to find him for a half hour before I finally did.'

Frank stood back gazing down at Carleton Whitsett, whose normally dandified appearance was gone, whose clothing was soiled, rumpled and torn. 'Is he dead?' Frank asked.

John went up close, knelt and looked into Whitsett's face. 'Not yet,' he said, back to Frank Arbuckle, and put forth his hand. Whitsett opened his eyes at the touch, looked John straight in the eyes and called him a fighting name in a soft and fading voice. Frank suddenly said, turning away from this scene, 'I'll tend to the others.' He called for their men across the creek to come on over and lend a hand at gathering up the guns and the dead for loading and hauling back down out of the mountains before the sun set on them all.

Whitsett seemed to realize his bitter feud was ended, for he rolled his head a little to watch Frank walk away, and said, 'I'll be back, Wheaton. I'll get over this wound and get more men and . . .'

'You better just lie easy,' the lawman told him. 'You want some water?'

Whitsett saw Lysle Small leaning upon his left leg back there, relaxed and hipshot. 'I should've sent them into the jailhouse after you,' he muttered, and called Lysle a hard name. 'I should've put a bigger bounty on you. Then they'd have gotten to you, law or no law, jailhouse an' guards, or no jailhouse an' guards.'

'Whitsett,' said John Wheaton. 'You concentrated on the wrong man. Lysle's only the rangeboss out at Big B. Jared Burcham's the owner.'

'You don't know how these things are done,' said Whitsett, rolling his cloudy eyes back towards Wheaton. 'You got to eliminate the rangebosses first. They're the toughest. I know. I've been through this plenty of times. You can break the owners with just one bullet from ambush, but first you got to eliminate their toughest men. I knew what . . . I was doing, Wheaton. I'd have got you too, if I'd just had another few days.'

'Why me, Whitsett?'

'Because a town without any law is the best kind of a town to take over. That's why.' Whitsett's throat filled up. A trickle of claret passed his lips and spilled downwards. He looked at it, for the first time seeming to realize just how badly he'd been hit. He raised his eyes, opening them wide with sudden realization, and fright. 'Wheaton . . . ?'

'It's pretty bad,' said John quietly. 'Lie easy an' we'll do what we can, Whitsett.'

But Whitsett's life was dissolving. He rocked his head limply from side to side and formed words with his lips which he lacked the power to utter, and finally he raised his eyes to accusingly stare over where Lysle was still standing in solemn silence. Then he gave a little shudder and collapsed inward—dead.

Finally, Lysle spoke, standing up straight and gazing at the man he'd killed. 'Why did he think he could do it, John? Everything was against him; numbers, firepower, even the law. He had to be a fool.'

John got stiffly to his feet, dusted his knees in silence and turned to watch Frank and their friends over there herding the prisoners all together to be searched for hideout weapons. 'They don't always fail,' he said quietly. 'And sometimes it seems that the crazier they are and the bigger their dream, the better their chances for success. This time, maybe, Whitsett just didn't aim high enough, or didn't plan hard enough.' He heaved a big sigh. 'Come on, Lysle; let's get the horses, get the dead ones lashed down and get out of here. I've been hungry so long I've almost forgotten what a decent meal would taste like.'

Lysle stood gazing down at Carleton Whitsett for a moment after Sheriff John Wheaton had strolled off, then he softly shook his head and also went away from that place.

Center Point Publishing
600 Brooks Road ● PO Box 1
Thorndike ME 04986-0001 USA

(207) 568-3717

US & Canada:
1 800 929-9108